LOVE CONQUERS ALL

A STAR LAKE ROMANCE #3

LORANA HOOPES

For my family - Thank you for letting me write the stories that fill my head.
For my friends - Thank you for your support and allowing me to watch you for inspiration.

NOTE FROM THE AUTHOR

This book is dear to my heart. I've always loved the small town feel and the crazy characters that generally live there. I hope you enjoy the story and the characters as they are dear to my heart. If you do, please leave a review at your retailer. It really does make a difference because it lets people make an informed decision about books.

Below are all the books in the small town series. I would love for you to check them out. I'd also like to offer you a sample of my newest book. Free Sample!

The Star Lake series:
When Love Returns

Once Upon A Star

Love Conquers All

LORANA HOOPES

A Star Lake Romance 3

Love
Conquers All

*L*anie Hall's footsteps echoed in the now half empty house. True to his word, Denny had cleared out his half of the furniture. The rusty orange recliner she had always hated? Gone. The glass topped coffee table she had always imagined children breaking and cutting themselves on? It was gone too. The fact they had never had kids to break the coffee table hadn't deterred her fears over the years.

All that remained of the living room furniture now was the couch her parents had given her when she first moved out. Faded and slightly stained, but otherwise in decent shape, it had lasted through college, and without kids, had held up well over the years as well.

Lanie wandered into the kitchen. Most of the appliances remained on the counter, but she noted the absence of the coffee pot. She might have to replace that as Denny's morning coffee habit had rubbed off on her some time in their ten years together.

With a heavy heart, Lanie followed the hallway into the bedroom which had felt empty for the last few years anyway. Somewhere around their fifth year of marriage, she and Denny had stopped touching and kissing. Forget sleeping in the same room at the same time. She would turn in and read a new book or get lost in a tv show until she fell asleep. He would fall asleep in the living room and leave for work without even saying goodbye. And that's how the last few years had passed.

Lanie crossed to the closet and opened the door. The small room had once been bursting with both their clothes, but now only hers hung on one side, creating a haphazard effect like a sinking ship. With a sigh she thought back to the last conversation she'd had with Denny.

"I can't do this anymore, Lanie. We hardly talk, and when

we do, it's short and curt. I want to experience something again."

"Let's try counseling, Denny," Lanie said, curling her hands against her legs. "I don't like feeling like roommates either."

"We could." Denny nodded and ran a hand through his short brown hair, "but I don't expect it would help. Neither of us is getting anything out of this marriage any longer. I think it best we go our separate ways."

Lanie blinked at him but nodded. A part of her had hoped he would fight, that he would agree to counseling or something else, but his adamant stance informed her he no longer cared to try. It saddened her a little, but she didn't have the energy to fight for them both.

She shut the closet door, hating the reminder of her failed marriage. Though the divorce wasn't official yet, it was only a matter of time. Denny was gone, and the paperwork was filed. As they hadn't wanted any of the same things and they planned on selling the house and splitting the profits, the smooth process had taken no time, and now she was simply playing the waiting game.

Suddenly, the house felt too empty, too condemning, and Lanie needed a break. She retraced her steps, grabbing her keys at the door, and hurried to her car. With no idea of where to go, she let her mind wander and her hands do the steering, but it wasn't much of a surprise when she pulled into Mic's, the radio station hang out.

It had been where she had spent many Friday nights, belting out karaoke until Denny decided he no longer wanted to go out. He had never insisted she not go, but there had been a silent request coupled with a heaping of guilt, and she had eventually stopped showing up.

Lanie paused with her hand on the door handle. What if this was no longer the hangout? What if she stepped inside and recognized no one there? Squaring her shoulders, she decided she didn't care. It couldn't be any worse or feel any lonelier than her empty house.

The darkened club looked exactly as she remembered if a little emptier, but a check of her wristwatch revealed the hour was still early. She sidled up to the bar for a drink, not because she was much of a drinker, but because she needed something to do.

"What'll you have?" the bartender asked. His bald pate contrasted with a full, thick beard, which formed an interesting contrast. Large gages created gaping holes in his ears, but his kind smile softened the hard image.

"Can I have a sprite please?"

The bartender raised one eyebrow at her, but turned and grabbed a glass.

"Lanie? Lanie Hall?"

Lanie looked to the left where the voice had come from, and her breath caught. Azarius Jacobson, a blast from her past, stood there dapper as ever in grey jeans and a darker grey shirt that accentuated his finely-toned arms.

They had once worked together at the radio station, though he had quit and done something else shortly after her marriage to Denny.

"Azarius? How have you been?" The words were barely out of her mouth before she threw her arms around him. They hadn't been close when he worked at the station years ago, but he was a familiar face on a day she needed one.

He chuckled as her weight knocked him a step backwards, and his arms surrounded her to keep them both from falling over.

Though purely innocent, she hadn't had a man's arms around her in so long that it ignited a flame deep inside her, and a heated flush crawled up her face as she registered his touch. "Sorry, I'm just excited to see someone I know, and I haven't seen you for what? Six years?"

"Eight," he said, dropping his arms. "You look fantastic. Just as I remembered."

Just as he remembered? The flush climbed higher up her face. She had only a vague memory of him from when he worked at the radio station, but he appeared to have a much better memory of her.

"You look great too. Why don't you get a drink and join me? I'd love to hear what you've been up to." Why did the simple thought of him joining her send her heart racing?

"Sure, I'd love to catch up with you."

He ordered a Vodka Tonic and led the way to an empty table.

"When did you get back to town?" she asked as they sat. The light above bounced off his dark skin, creating a glittering caramel effect.

"About six months ago," he said. "I'm not working for the radio station this time though."

She smiled as she sipped her soda. "I figured you weren't. I'm still there, and I would have noticed if you were back."

"Would you have?" His dark brown eyes bored into her soul, and she dropped her eyes and bit her lip.

"Honestly, I don't know," she said, stirring her straw in a circle. "Things have been crazy."

"Oh yeah? What's been going on?"

His gaze never wavered from her, and the intensity of it sent a shiver down her spine. When was the last time someone had looked at her like that? As if he really saw her? Years, she decided. It had been years, and the simple act not only made her feel beautiful but lowered her emotional walls.

"My marriage fell apart," she sighed. "I guess it had been going that direction for awhile, but we finally decided to stop fighting the lack of feelings and call it quits."

"I'm sorry to hear that," he said, but something about his expression made her wonder if he really were sorry.

"So, what about you?" she asked, changing the subject. Her failed marriage was a topic she wanted to forget, not rehash. "How has life been for you?"

He shrugged. "It's been. I re-enlisted for awhile. You knew I was National Guard, right?"

Lanie blinked and shook her head. She'd had no idea he was in the service. Wow, she really had been clueless about him. That was a pretty big piece of information to miss about someone.

"Oh, well I needed a change, so I re-enlisted for a

few years. My time just ended, so I'm back here as a civilian again, doing some contract work."

The shifting of his eyes led her to believe there was more to the story, but she didn't press the issue. It felt like prying and that seemed rude after not having seen him for so long.

"Do you sing?" she asked, gesturing at the karaoke book on the table in an attempt to change the conversation.

A small smile pulled at the corner of his lips. "No, but I'd love to hear you sing. I always enjoyed watching you belting it out in the booth."

Unsure how to respond to that tidbit of information, Lanie felt her face flush again. Had Azarius had a crush on her? If so, did he still? And did she want him to? These questions circled through her brain, but all she could manage was, "You watched me?"

"Only a few times," he said. "You always looked like you were having fun, so go ahead and pick something. I'll cheer you on."

Azarius kicked himself as Lanie's auburn head dropped to scan the binder of songs. He had almost spilled how attracted he was to her. He had been for years. In fact, her marriage was what drove him from the station and to re-enlist. Though he'd never gotten up the nerve to tell her how he felt, seeing her married to another had been unbearable.

Now here they were back in the same town and both single. He finally had the chance to show her how he felt, if he didn't mess it up too badly.

"Okay, I think I'll try this one." Lanie pointed to a song in the book.

He smiled and nodded at her as she scribbled the choice on a piece of paper. Azarius didn't care what she sang; she had the voice of an angel any time she opened her mouth.

Lanie stood and made her way to the stage, handing over the piece of paper to the DJ. He scanned it and motioned for her to take the mic on the small raised platform that served as a stage. Looking a little timid, she stood in front of the microphone and offered him a small smile.

Azarius flashed her a thumbs up and smiled as the music started. She probably had no idea the Duran Duran song she chose reminded him of her. He thought back to the day he had accidentally stumbled upon her singing it in the booth.

· · ·

"**A**zarius, can you look at the board in control room three?" the station manager asked. "It's been frizzing out again."

"Of course, sir," Azarius said. He grabbed the tool box from the closet that housed it and headed downstairs to the control booths. Lanie was on in control room three, which made the job even more appealing. Azarius didn't believe in love at first sight, but from the moment he had met Lanie, she had affected him in a way no other woman had. Now if he could just get up the courage to tell her.

Duran Duran's "Come Undone" was billowing out of the room as he approached. He knocked on the door, but when the music didn't lower, he assumed she hadn't heard his knock, and he pushed the door open slowly.

Lanie stood behind the board in a pair of cutoff denim shorts and a red tank top. Her auburn hair flowed freely down her shoulders and bounced with the movement of her head from side to side.

Her beautiful soprano voice belted out the lyrics, mesmerizing Azarius. He could have stood there all day watching her. "Can I believe you're taking my... Oh!" Her voice stopped as she turned and spied him standing there. "I'm sorry, I didn't hear you come in."

"That's okay." He smiled and held up the tool box, so she would realize he wasn't being voyeuristic. "I knocked but ..." he shrugged. "I need to check out the control panel."

She lowered the music and stepped back. "Of course. You have about two minutes until this song ends though."

"I'll be quick."

"I love singing," she said as if trying to explain her actions. "And since the booth is soundproof, I often test my range since no one can hear me. My singing doesn't go out over the radio."

Azarius bit his lip to hide his smile at her nervousness. "Even if it did, no one would mind," he said. "You have a beautiful voice." He watched the soft pink color climb her face before turning back to the control panel.

"W as it okay?" Lanie asked as she finished the song and returned to the table.

"It was amazing," Azarius said.

A rose color flooded Lana's cheeks, and she dropped her eyes. "You don't have to say that."

"No, I don't, but you are an amazing singer." Her eyes lifted, and he felt himself falling into the hazel depths. "Lanie, I'd love to hang out with you again," he began. "Are you into eighties music?"

Lanie blinked at him. "Am I into what?"

"Eighties music. I know it sounds silly, but I love to watch old music videos, and I thought maybe you'd like to hang out and watch them with me."

"Like a date?" she asked, one eyebrow arched in the air.

Azarius realized how silly that sounded. Yeah, come hang out and watch videos with me, but it was who he was. "Like two old friends reconnecting," he said. "With the possibility of more."

She smiled at him and placed her hand on his, sending tingles down his arm. "I'd like that. I could use an old friend right about now."

CHAPTER 2

*A*zarius walked through his two-bedroom apartment looking for any mess he may have missed. He was generally a neat person, but on laundry day he had a habit of throwing the clothes in his oversized chair where they stayed until the sight bothered him enough he put them away. Thankfully, today hadn't been laundry day and everything appeared to be put away and neat.

A knock sounded at the door moments later. Lanie stood on the other side in a brown sweater and jeans. Her hands were shoved in her jean pockets as if nervous.

"Hey, come on in." Azarius stepped back and opened the door for her.

"Thanks." As she stepped over the threshold, her

eyes darted left and right, taking in the small living room. "Nice place."

Azarius shrugged. "It's nothing much, but it works for me. Would you like something to drink?"

"Sure, I'll take water."

As she wandered around the room, taking in the pictures on his walls, he darted into the small kitchen to fill her a glass. When he returned, she was staring at a picture of his mother and her family.

"That's my mother, her husband, and my sisters." Azarius laughed when Lanie's eyebrows knitted together at the difference in their skin color. "My adopted mother."

"I had no idea you were adopted," she said.

"Yeah, my mama was taken from me way too young, but my mother and I are close." He hoped she wouldn't ask about his mama. Though he might tell her one day, it was not a story he shared often.

"I always considered adoption special anyway because you know your parents really wanted you."

Azarius had never thought about it like that, but it did make sense, and while his memories of his mama were hazy, he was close to his mother.

"Yeah, I guess you're right. Here's your water. You wanna have a seat?"

Lanie nodded and chose an edge of the couch.

He opted for the opposite edge, leaving enough space between them they weren't immediately touching though he longed to feel her warmth against him. Reaching behind him, he grabbed the remote and flicked on the TV.

"Now you get to see how I spend my nights," he said with a laugh. "YouTube," he said into the remote and his video log popped up.

"Your remote is voice activated?" Lanie asked, her eyes wide.

He nodded. "You got a favorite eighties song?"

"Um." She pursed her lips and closed her eyes, creating just the tiniest of wrinkles across her forehead. "'The Wild Wild West' by Escape Club."

Azarius had never heard of the song, but he repeated the name into the remote and a video lit up the screen.

"Oh my gosh, that is so weird," Lanie said as a pair of lips filled the screen.

"You've never seen this before?"

Lanie shook her head, a smile on her face. "We never had cable growing up, so I only heard it on the radio. I don't think I would have liked it as much if I had seen the video," she laughed.

"Well, then close your eyes," he said.

Lanie shut her lids and began singing along with

the video. Azarius's attention shifted from the TV to Lanie. He could listen to her sing all day. The movement of her lips garnered his attention, and he fought the urge to kiss her. As her head moved slightly to the music and her voice filled his ears, he realized he wanted more moments like this with her.

Lanie couldn't believe how much fun she was having watching old music videos with Azarius. His taste in music matched hers to a T, at least when it came to old songs, and there was something comforting about hanging out with him.

"You hungry?" he asked. "We could go get dinner."

Her stomach rumbled in answer. "Yeah, I guess I am."

Azarius stood and held out his hand to help Lanie up from the couch. She placed her hand in his, enjoying the soft feel of his skin against hers. As he pulled her up, she lost her footing and fell into his chest, her hands splaying across his muscles. She had deduced he worked out, but his chest was solid and well-formed. His arms wrapped around her waist to steady her, and for a moment Lanie thought he might kiss her.

She found the thought exciting and terrifying at the same time. Though she couldn't deny she was beginning to feel something for Azarius, she wasn't sure it was appropriate. After all, Denny had moved out only a few days ago, but it had been much longer since there had been romantic feelings between them. In fact, she couldn't remember the last time she had been in Denny's arms like this.

"Sorry," Lanie said, dropping her eyes.

"Don't be."

Azarius removed his arms, and Lanie immediately missed the warmth of his touch and then felt guilty for it. *What is going on with me?*

"Shall we take my car?" Azarius asked.

Lanie nodded, curious about his Mustang and not trusting her voice. Did he see the effect he was having on her?

She followed him through the kitchen to the small garage where his lime green Mustang took up most of the footage. A washer and dryer and some shelves filled the rest of it.

Azarius opened the passenger door for her and Lanie slid into the black leather seat. She'd never been in his car, but she had seen plenty of posts of it on Instagram.

He slid into the driver's side beside her and punched the garage door opener.

"You ready?" he asked, flashing her a smile as he donned a pair of large grey shades. They resembled old cop glasses, but they didn't look silly on his face.

"Ready for what?" Lanie asked as she fastened her seatbelt.

"This is a turbo," he said with a mischievous smile, "and I like to go fast."

The engine hummed to life and Azarius backed the car out. As soon as he shifted into drive though, the car zoomed forward and Lanie shot back against the seat. Her hand flew to the handle above the door, and she held on for dear life.

A few minutes later, she was thrown forward as Azarius parked.

"Do you always drive like that?" Lanie asked, trying to calm her racing heart. Her hand was still firmly fastened around the "oh crud" handle.

Azarius laughed as he plucked the key from the ignition and opened the driver door.

Before Lanie could open her door, he had come around the side, opened it for her, and held his hand out to help her up.

Lanie took his hand, thankful for the support as she stood on wobbly legs. He didn't drop her hand as she expected, but instead laced his fingers through hers. Something about the clash of his dark skin against her fair skin caused her heart to flutter.

"This is my favorite sandwich shop," he said, holding the door open for her. His eyes danced like a kid's at Christmas time, eliciting a small laugh from Lanie as they entered the quaint establishment.

An elder teen stood below an enlarged menu and behind the cash register. "Welcome to Johnie's, what can I get you?" The monotonous timbre of his voice matched his expressionless face.

"I recommend the number two." Azarius focused on Lanie, ignoring the boy behind the counter, "but you order what you want."

Lanie smiled at the employee, whose name tag read Brad, and scanned the large menu. She had been hoping to start eating healthier - she'd packed on a few extra pounds in the last year from lack of exercise and feeling undesired. Ordering a salad felt wrong somehow though, and the number two did look delicious if they could hold the onions.

"I'll take his recommendation, but can I get it without the onions?" Cooked onions were fine, but raw ones never agreed with her stomach. Plus, she didn't like the spicy taste in her mouth or the way her breath smelled afterwards.

"Sure." Blank-faced Brad punched a button in the register and shifted his eyes to Azarius.

"You don't know what you're missing," Azarius said, dropping her hand as he crossed his arms and leaned back. "Am I right, man?"

Brad shrugged, and Lanie bit her lip together to keep from laughing.

"Well, I think the onions make the sandwich," Azarius said. "So you can add her onions to mine."

"That's not the way it works," Brad said with a minute shake of his head.

"It's okay, he's only kidding," Lanie smirked.

"No, I'm not. They can smother mine with onions," Azarius continued. "And I'll take a big bowl of the chili. It's delicious here. In fact, you can throw more onions on the chili."

"But we don't…" Brad began.

"Don't worry about it," Lanie said, trying to keep from busting out laughing. "He's giving you a hard time." She'd never seen this playful side of Azarius. "Behave; he doesn't get paid enough to deal with you," she said.

Brad punched another few buttons and glanced

up. "Will that be all?" His voice finally registered emotion - an impatient desire to be done with them.

"I'm good," Lanie said.

"Yep, I guess we're good," Azarius said, reaching for his wallet.

"That will be $21.43 then."

"Oh, I can pay for mine," Lanie said, patting her pocket.

Azarius fished two bills out and placed them on the counter. "No, I got this, but you're an expensive date," he said, winking at Lanie.

"Hah, I only ordered a sandwich. The rest was all you," she said, swatting at his arm.

He caught her hand and held it to his chest, sending a shiver up her arm. Time seemed to slow as their eyes locked. Did this mean he had feelings for her too?

"Ahem," Brad cleared his throat, breaking the connection. "Your change."

"Oh, right, thank you." Azarius scooped up the bills and stuffed them back in his wallet. The small amount of change he dropped in a glass jar on the counter that sported a "give a penny, take a penny" sign.

Lanie's hand tingled from the recent touch, and

she wandered over to a window to process her feelings.

It felt wrong to be having romantic feelings for Azarius, but it had been ages since she had felt anything romantic for Denny, and he had never looked at her the way Azarius did - as if she were the most beautiful woman in the world.

"You ready?" Azarius asked, holding the bag of food up. It was an innocuous question, but the look in his eyes made her wonder if a second meaning existed in the innocent question.

Lanie nodded and followed him out to the car.

CHAPTER 3

*A*zarius shut the door after Lanie left and sighed with relief. Spending the evening with her was even better than he had imagined it would be. She hadn't laughed at his video watching habit, and she had enjoyed his favorite dinner, even if she did ruin it by leaving the onions off. Best of all, she had agreed to come back again. It had taken eight years, but Azarius finally felt as if he'd be able to show her his true feelings.

As he collapsed on the couch and flicked the television on for a reminder of the evening – "Wild Wild West" would now forever remind him of her - his phone rang.

"Hello?" he asked, punching the button. It couldn't be Lanie as they hadn't exchanged numbers yet. He preferred his privacy and didn't share his number with most people though he figured he would share it with Lanie soon.

"Az?"

Azarius stifled a sigh as he recognized his friend, Greg's voice. He liked Greg; after all he'd been there for Azarius when Krista left, but Greg didn't always have his life together. If he was calling, it was probably because he wanted something.

"Hey, Greg, what's up?"

"Not much man, just checking in to see how life is treating you."

Azarius knew this was a soft opening to see what mood he was in before Greg laid out his request, but spending the evening with Lanie left him so elated he decided to play along. "Life is good. I spent the evening with a lovely woman."

"Alright, Az," Greg said.

"Not like that, man. We just hung out. This girl's special."

"Special, huh? I can't remember the last time you called a girl special."

"Yeah, it's been a while." Azarius didn't want to ask the question, but he knew it was coming whether he asked or not. "So, how is life for you?"

"It's not bad, but uh, my sister's baby is due in a

few weeks and she needs me to find another place to stay. I hate to ask, but it'll probably only be for a few weeks. I'll find another place as soon as I can. So, can I come stay with you?"

And there it was! Azarius wanted to say no. The last thing he needed was Greg hanging around cramping his style or scaring Lanie away, but he had been there for Azarius when he was at his lowest. Azarius owed him.

"Sure, man. I mean if it's only for a few weeks. You know I like my space."

"Awesome. Yeah, a few weeks, a month or two at the most."

Azarius rolled his eyes. This would probably end in disaster, but he'd already agreed. "Can you wait another week at least?" That would give him time to see Lanie a few more times before introducing Greg.

"Yeah, Cheryl will probably give me a week. I appreciate this man, more than you know."

Azarius doubted that, but the wheels were already set in motion.

"What's up?" Lanie asked, touching Azarius' shoulder. "You've seemed distracted all night."

He tapped his index finger against his lips. "Are you having fun hanging out with me?"

"Of course I am," she said. She hadn't told him how much she was enjoying it, but she couldn't imagine not seeing him once or twice a week.

"Would you still enjoy it if there was someone else here?"

Lanie furrowed her brow, not understanding his cryptic question. "What do you mean? Like hanging out with us or just sitting here staring at us?"

"Not really hanging out with us, but here. I have a friend I owe a favor to who needs a place to stay. He's moving in at the end of the week."

"Well, that's nice of you," Lanie said. "Are you going to be okay with a full-time roommate?" It was a question that had plagued her the last few days. Azarius seemed set in his ways and a fan of routines just so, which made her wonder if he'd ever be ready for a real relationship. Not that she was ready to jump into anything full-time, but eventually she wanted to marry again and that meant living together and sharing a space.

The corner of his lip pulled into a small smile. "I

honestly don't know. I haven't lived with anyone in ages. I'm pretty happy having my own space."

"Yeah, I figured that about you, but I still think it's nice of you to help your friend out." Plus, maybe it would let Lanie know if he'd ever be able to marry. Marriage? She wasn't looking for marriage. Her own divorce wasn't even final yet. What was wrong with her?

"So, it won't bother you? We could always hang out upstairs if he gets too annoying or lock him in his room."

Lanie chuckled and batted his arm. "Any friend of yours is a friend of mine. It will be fine." *Kind of like having a chaperone*, she added to herself. Nothing other than holding hands had occurred, but if she kept coming over, she knew something might.

"Good. Now let's jam some."

He turned up the television, stood, and held out a hand to her. West End Girls blared out of the big screen. Not the best song to dance to, but Lanie didn't mind.

Azarius twirled her around as if they were waltzing, smiling as he did. Lanie leaned her head back and laughed. She couldn't remember the last time she felt so free or so comfortable.

❦

L anie stared at the silent phone and bit her thumbnail. It had been days since she'd heard from Azarius. She knew he was probably busy with his roommate, but his lack of communication reignited old fears. Maybe she had misread him and he didn't have feelings for her. Maybe he just needed a friend and now that he had a roommate, she was no longer needed.

Lanie hated this insecurity that plagued her. Growing up in an ice cream parlor with a sweet tooth had kept her from being a skinny kid. While she had managed to lose most of the weight when she got to college, she still often felt like the fat little girl. It was one reason she believed she had accepted Denny's marriage proposal when she did. Sure, she thought she had loved him, but she also feared there might not be another proposal, and so she'd said yes even though there had been a few moments of doubt early in their relationship.

Now, she was facing the same doubt but for different reasons. Azarius was an enigma. He hadn't asked for her number, nor had he offered his own, saying he preferred to chat through instant messenger. Lanie hadn't minded at first, but now she wondered if it was so he could ignore her when he wanted. After all, it was harder to ignore a ringing phone than a text message.

She didn't want to be the one texting him again, but she did want to see him. The indecision plagued her another few minutes before she swallowed her pride and tapped out a message to him. *-Just saying hi and wondering how your day went.-* Yeah, that seemed innocent enough. If he didn't respond, she would know he was no longer interested.

Lanie hit the send button and stared at the blue box of text, willing a reply to come through. She had almost given up hope when the phone vibrated in her hand.

-Hey you, my day was good. Where have you been?-

Where had she been? She'd sent the last text a few days ago and then nothing. Shaking her head, she texted out a reply. *-I've been okay. Wondering where you were since I sent the last text.-*

She bit her thumbnail again as she waited for his reply.

-I'm sorry. My phone has been messing up lately, and I haven't been getting all my texts.-

His answer soothed her ego though it didn't calm all of her old fears. *-Want to hang out tonight?-* He was always easier to read in person.

-Yeah, but the roommate will be here.-

The corners of Lanie's lips pulled into a smile. She didn't care if the roommate was there as long as she got to see Azarius. "See you about eight."

There was no new car in the driveway when she pulled in that night, which made Lanie wonder if perhaps the roommate was out after all.

She rang the bell, expecting Azarius to be on the other side, but when it swung open, a skinny white man with a goatee stood facing her. His stare caught Lanie off guard slightly and she rocked back on her heels.

"Hi, I'm Lanie. Is Azarius home?"

The man stepped back. "He's upstairs."

Lanie had expected an introduction in return, but the man shut the door behind her and plopped back down on the couch where he must have been when she knocked. With a slight shake of her head, she mounted the stairs. Azarius was the one she was here to see anyway.

His door was shut, and she knocked gently before pushing it open. Azarius lay on his bed in the dark.

The only light was from the television, which was of course playing music videos.

"Hey, come join me," he said, patting the bed beside him.

Lanie hesitated momentarily. Though they had yet to even kiss, she knew accidents often happened when beds were involved, but he looked so out of sorts that she threw caution to the wind and climbed in beside him, leaving a small sliver of space in between them.

"What's up? You look miserable," Lanie said.

"He's so loud," Azarius said.

"Who?"

"Greg, my roommate. I thought I could handle having someone else here, but he's driving me crazy."

Lanie chuckled. "It's only been a few days, Az, I'm sure you'll get used to it."

"I don't know. I like being able to do my own thing, and he's crimping my style."

His words reminded Lanie of a fear she had been battling. "Do you think you'd ever be able to live with a woman then, a wife?"

"I don't know," he said, leveling his gaze at her. "I might have to have my own house, a getaway."

"Wouldn't that defeat the purpose though?"

He shrugged. "Maybe if it were the right woman, it wouldn't matter."

Lanie tried to tell herself it didn't matter if she weren't the right woman. They were just friends after all, weren't they? She was no longer sure. Though she had tried to quash her feelings for him, every time she was around him, they grew stronger.

He opened his arm and pulled her against him. Lanie could feel his heart beat beneath her palm. "When is your birthday?"

"Why?" he asked.

"Because I'm curious," Lanie asked. In reality, she wanted some piece of him. So far, everything he had shared had been superficial. She knew he liked eighties music and working out. She knew where he lived and what he drove, but she didn't know much else about him, and it was starting to worry her.

"It doesn't matter," he said. His eyes stayed glued to the television but his arm tightened around her.

"It does to me," she said, reaching up and turning his face to hers. "I want to know you, Azarius, like really know you."

He returned her gaze, but instead of answering with words, he leaned closer and placed his lips on hers. Fire burned through her at his touch, and for the moment, it didn't matter.

CHAPTER 4

*A*s the weeks continued to fly by, winter's icy talons faded to the first buds of spring. Though Lanie always felt connected to Azarius when they were together, doubts would creep in when they were apart. If only he would open up to her, then perhaps she could quell the thoughts that haunted her when her phone remained silent.

On the way to his house that evening, Lanie realized he had never been to her house. Though she didn't mind hanging at his place - there were no memories of a failed marriage there - she did wonder why he'd never even asked to come to her house, especially with Greg at his place. Not that Greg ever bothered them. Most of the time he excused himself and went upstairs as soon as Lanie arrived.

The lights in the house were dark when Lanie pulled into the drive. She checked her watch. 8:05, five minutes later than she said she'd be there. Lanie fired off an instant message, but no reply came. Perhaps he was resting upstairs. Azarius had often told her to come on in if the door was unlocked.

With the engine off, the surrounding stillness blanketed her. Would the neighbors think she was breaking in? She'd never spoken with any of them, but surely they would recognize her car by now.

She rang the bell, feeling more conspicuous as the seconds ticked by. When no lights came on, she tried the knob. It turned in her hand, and she ventured inside. The living room was completely dark, and Lanie wasn't sure where the light switch was.

As she fumbled with the flashlight feature on her phone, a light in the kitchen flicked on. Lanie jumped, nearly dropping her phone, before she realized it was Greg. He stood against the far counter, a bottle of milk in between his feet.

"Greg, it's me Lanie," she said when he made no motion to greet her.

"Lanie?" Though not slurred, it was clear he had been drinking by the way he said her name.

"Yeah, is Azarius home?"

Greg shook his head as he bent over and retrieved the milk container from the floor. "I don't know where he's at, but you're welcome to wait."

Lanie bit her lip as the refrigerator door opened and closed. She did want to see Azarius, but she had never been alone with Greg, and she wasn't sure she trusted him. "Um, maybe I'll just see if he answers a call." She punched in his number, but as it rang in her ear, a light flashed on the back of the couch and she realized his phone sat there charging. Well, at least that explained why he hadn't responded to her text.

"He gave you his number?" Greg asked as he entered the living room. Dark circles ringed his eyes and the wrinkled t-shirt and sweats he wore appeared as if he'd slept in them all day.

"Um, yeah, finally," Lanie said, ending the call. "Why is he so secretive about it anyway?"

Greg shrugged and sat down on the end of the couch. "He just is. I won't talk bad about my brother. I mean he's not my real brother, but you know what I mean."

Lanie nodded and sat at the other end of the couch. "I wasn't asking you to speak ill of him."

"He likes you though." Greg's tone was so

nonchalant Lanie almost missed the words, and rather than look at her, he flicked on the television.

"How do you know?" Lanie asked, wishing she had his undivided attention, but determined to fish for whatever information she could get.

Another shrug. "I just know. He's different around you. I haven't seen him that way since..." He snapped his mouth shut, and Lanie knew there was more to the story.

"Why doesn't he ever tell me then?"

Greg shook his head, keeping his lips sealed.

With a small sigh, Lanie turned her attention to the television, hoping Greg would open up again. "Does he talk about me?" she asked.

"A little. I know you're still married."

"Only on paper," Lanie said. "Denny's moved out, and I haven't even heard from him since he left. The paperwork should be finalized any day now."

"How serious are you?"

The intensity of the question caught Lanie off guard and she paused before answering. She believed she loved Azarius, but the secrecy he held kept her from falling completely. There were times she could imagine a life with him and other times she believed he would change his mind one day and she would be left alone, again.

"I could be serious," she said. "If I knew he was."

"What makes you think he's not?" Greg asked.

"He never asks me over," Lanie said, dropping her eyes to her hands. She had never voiced that insecurity out loud, and she couldn't believe she had told Greg, a near stranger. "I always have to ask him if he wants to see me. I just want to know he wants me. I told him that the other night and you know what he did?"

"No, what?"

"He sent me a Nine Inch Nails video. No explanation, just this video. Then he told me to listen to it."

"Which one?" Greg asked, sitting up straighter.

"'Dead Souls.' It's from the movie The Crow. He asked me if I got it, and I tried but I didn't see how the words applied to us. I told him I liked the movie, how The Crow would do anything for the woman he loved, and he just replied with 'It means everything.' Why can't he just tell me how he feels?"

"Az marches to a different drum," Greg said with a smile, "but don't give up on him. It's not my place to say anything, but there's a reason he's the way he is and believe it or not, him telling you 'It means everything' is his way of telling you he cares."

The whir of the garage door ended the conversation.

"This conversation never happened," Greg said and Lanie nodded. Telling Azarius of the conversation wouldn't help her position anyway.

She stood as the door to the garage opened and Azarius appeared in the kitchen. "You stayed. I was so afraid I would miss you," he said, stepping toward Lanie.

"Where were you?" Lanie crossed her arms to keep from running into his. "I told you I was coming."

"I know," he sighed. "A friend called asking for help to set some things up. I thought I would be done in time, but traffic was bad and my friend was very talkative. I'm sorry."

His eyes looked sincere, and though his answer was vague, Lanie weighed it with Greg's words and figured it was as good as she was going to get. He took another step toward her, asking permission to touch her with his eyes. At least he recognized she was angry.

Sighing, she closed the distance and felt his arms wrap around her. If only she could stay here, in his arms where she felt warm and loved.

Azarius wasn't expecting the knock that came at six that night. He had just gotten home and was hoping to change clothes and hit the gym before Lanie came by.

When he opened the front door, Lanie stood on the other side with wild eyes and a dazed expression. "Sorry I didn't call first. Can I come in?"

"Of course. You know you're always welcome."

He closed the door behind her and grabbed her upper arms. The look on her face scared him. He'd never seen her so frazzled.

"It's official," she said and then laughed or snorted; he wasn't sure which.

"What's official?" He felt like he had missed some crucial piece of information.

"My divorce." She held up a paper he hadn't even seen clutched tightly in her hand.

"Ah." He knew this feeling. Even though he and Krista had been separated for years before she filed, the final proclamation that his marriage was over had hit him similarly. "It's going to be okay," he said, moving his arms to the back of her waist.

Before he could say another word, she leaned up

and covered her lips with his own. He responded, enjoying the soft feel of her mouth, until the intensity changed. Emotions he had never experienced from Lanie poured into him and with all his energy, he pushed her back.

"Lanie, not like this. You're hurting, and you're not thinking straight." Though he wanted to be intimate with her, she had often said she wouldn't have sex outside of marriage. It was one reason he didn't kiss her as much as he wanted to because he was afraid if he started, he might not be able to honor her wishes.

Instead of words, her reply was another fevered kiss. Her hands locked around his neck, and though he knew they'd probably both regret it in the morning, he let her lead him up the stairs and to his bed.

When Azarius woke the next morning, he sensed something was missing before he even opened his eyes. His hand reached out, but the place where Lanie should have been was empty and cold.

He forced his eyes open, but the room was empty.

On the other pillow lay a white piece of paper. 'I'm sorry' was all it said, but somehow Azarius knew it was more than an apology for last night. In the pit of his stomach he suspected he had lost her for good, and a darkness descended upon him.

CHAPTER 5

*L*anie Perkins Hall stared at the two-story house she had once called home and sighed. Coming home felt like a failure and not at all how she imagined her life at thirty. At this point, she was supposed to be married with three kids - two boys and a girl or two girls and a boy. Instead, she found herself divorced, childless, alone, and back in Star Lake where single men were as prevalent as four-leaf clovers, but she hadn't known where to turn after last night.

She had spent the morning avoiding Azarius's calls while she hired a moving company and a realtor to sell the house. Her final stop before making the trip home was the radio station where she requested a leave of absence. It wasn't normally done, but Lanie had been such a staple at the station for so long that the manager had agreed to give her six months to sort her life out and decide what she wanted to do.

With that chapter of her life mostly closed - she'd have to deal with Azarius at some point - she packed a few bags, threw them in her car, and pointed it to the last place she had felt grounded: Star Lake.

With a sigh, she turned the engine off and popped the trunk. Inside was a small suitcase with some clothes and toiletries, her tablet, and a few books. The rest of her furniture and clothes would arrive later.

"Lanie, you're here!" Her mother's voice carried from the porch where she stood waving. Lanie shut the trunk and grabbed her purse from the passenger side before mounting the few steps to join her mother, an older, plumper version of herself.

"Hi, Mom. Thanks for letting me crash here a few days while I find a place."

"We couldn't leave you on the street, honey, and don't worry about a place." She held the door open for Lanie to enter. "You can stay here as long as you'd like."

Lanie forced a smile and swallowed her reply. If she had anywhere else to go, she wouldn't be crashing with her parents. Though she loved them, they were easier to tolerate in smaller doses like at Christmas or Thanksgiving. If she'd planned better, she could have rented a room at the inn, but spring was Layla's busiest time, and Lanie didn't want to be an inconvenience.

"Dad is watching TV if you want to stop in and say hi."

"Can I drop my bag off first?" Lanie asked. Elaine, her mother, was easy to get along with, but her father was another matter. Ex-military, Bob had always been strict, and he hadn't jumped for joy when she moved away or when she married Denny. He'd be even more disappointed if he learned about her latest indiscretion, but she hoped never to have that discussion with him.

Her mother seemed to understand the hesitation as she nodded and ran her hands over the faded apron across her front. "I'll be in the kitchen. When you get settled in, come and join me."

"Thanks, Mother." Lanie continued down the familiar hallway to her old bedroom. A faded patch stood out in the middle of the door where her "Danger! Moody Teenager" sign used to hang. The door opened, revealing a room decorated in pink and beige. That hadn't been the way it had looked in high school, but after she moved out, her mother had removed the posters, re-painted the walls, and mellowed the color scheme. Lanie couldn't blame her. While John Stamos had aged well, he was no longer the teen heartthrob he had been at one time.   Lanie set her suitcase on the floor and plopped down on the full-size bed. It wasn't as comfortable as her own bed, but it would do for the few days she planned to be here. House hunting was in her immediate future.

She lay back and regarded the ceiling, wishing she didn't have to greet her father. Not that she didn't love him, but he was a ritualistic Christian who didn't believe in divorce. While she didn't either, sometimes life didn't turn out as planned. She certainly hadn't planned last night, and she'd asked repeatedly for forgiveness. Still, she wondered if the guilt would ever leave her. With a sigh, she pushed herself off the bed and prepared to face the music.   True to form, her father occupied the old recliner and faced the television. A home improvement show blared back at him. For as long as memory served her, this was how he spent his evenings. Elaine would cook, they would eat, and then her father would retire to the living room. Lanie wondered if her parents loved each other any longer or if they had decided being roommates was enough after such a long time together.

"Hi, Dad." Lanie perched on the tan couch, ready to flee if he became too disagreeable.

"Hello, Lanie." An eye flick her direction, but words cool as ice. "You couldn't try counseling, huh?"

"It wasn't all my decision, Dad. Denny didn't want to try counseling. What was I supposed to do, beg?"

"Pray, for one."

"I prayed, Dad, but it didn't work out." Lanie tried to hide her exasperation at her father not hearing her words.

"What are you planning for employment?" he asked, changing the subject.

"I'm not sure yet. Being a disc jockey was fun, but no radio station exists around here, and even if one did, I doubt the pay would be enough." Lanie had thought little about work, but the question gave her pause. There weren't many skills in her arsenal. Radio had been her passion in college and had become her career. A few odd jobs existed in her past, but nothing boasting much talent.

"Work at the store," he suggested. "I'm getting

older and would like to spend more time at home. I'd always hoped you would take it over."

This was not new information. Her father had been pushing for her to run the shop since she was sixteen, and while it wasn't where she wanted to end up permanently, it would solve her immediate employment issues and give her a steady income while she decided what she wanted to do with the rest of her life. "I can do that, Dad. I can't guarantee I'll take it over, but I'll help until I decide what I want to do next."

His sniff showed his annoyance that she was still not following his footsteps, but he kept the thought to himself. "Fine then," was all he said.

Lanie rolled her eyes, wondering if she and her father would ever have a better relationship. "I wonder if Mom needs any help," she said, standing and moving toward the exit.

Her father nodded as she exited the room and made her way to the kitchen where her mother was finishing cleaning. A neatnik, her mother never retired for the night until the kitchen was spotless.

"Up for a game?" Elaine asked.

Lanie and her mother had often passed the time playing card games when Lanie was growing up.

"Sure, how about some Yahtzee?" Lanie pulled

out a barstool and sat down across from her mother. Though she hadn't played in ages–Denny had never been interested–Lanie enjoyed the challenge.

Lanie woke the next morning as the first rays of light peeked in her window. A visit to Layla, her high school chum, was on her docket before approaching the realtor to see what was available. After pulling on a pair of jeans and a shirt, she ran a brush through her hair and headed to the kitchen for some coffee and cereal.

Her father sat at the table, a mug on his right and his Bible open in front of him. He read it every morning before work without fail. Lanie wished she had his passion for studying the important book, but some days, even though she knew she should, she couldn't get into it. Her lack of being in the word probably had a lot to do with her slip as well.

"Will you be able to work the evening shift tonight?" he asked without looking up.

Lanie stifled a sigh as she pulled a mug from the cupboard. Couldn't he have started with a 'good morning' at least? "Yeah, Dad, I should be able to. I'm visiting the realtor today hoping to find a house to rent, but I should finish by four. Will that work?"

"We close at eight," he said, looking up at her. "That's a short shift."

Lanie bit her lip as she poured the coffee. She didn't want to start the morning by fighting with her father. "It's just for today, Dad. Once I have a place rented, I can start earlier, okay?"

His hazel eyes regarded her, and just like when she was younger, she shrunk under the gaze. How did he make her feel small even at age thirty?

"I suppose it will have to do," he said, as his eyes dropped back to the Bible.

With a shake of her head, Lanie took a sip of her coffee and decided to get breakfast out. She no longer felt like sitting even for a bowl of cereal.

Another few large gulps of coffee sent enough caffeine through her system she assumed she could make it until she found more. Max served coffee at The Diner, and she had seen a new bakery on her drive in which might have an even better option. She rinsed the cup in the sink and placed it in the dish rack.

"Tell Mom I'll be back later," Lanie called as she headed for the front door, grabbing a light jacket on the way. Without even bothering to pull it on, she opened the door and stepped outside.

Though nearing summer, an unusual chill nipped at her light jacket, sending a shiver down her spine as she closed the door behind her. She jammed her hands in the sleeves and snuggled down into the jacket as she zipped it up. The keys jingled in her right pocket, and she retrieved them as she walked to the car. It wasn't a long walk into town, but it was a little too cold for the jaunt today, especially since she had left without her scarf and gloves.

The cold leather seats had barely warmed up when she parked the car in front of the Star Lake Inn.

"Lanie," Layla shrieked as she entered the foyer.

Lanie smiled as her high school friend came around the desk and enveloped her in a hug. "Hey, Layla. You look great." Layla always looked good. With her long dark hair and blue eyes, she had been the focus of the boys in high school, though her eyes had only been on Max and the rumor was they had finally gotten together.

"You do too," Layla said, stepping back to inspect Lanie.

"I'm okay," Lanie said, rolling her eyes. "I need to increase my gym time."

"Oh pooh, you look amazing. Now you need a man."

Lanie shook her head, remembering the last night before she left. It wasn't an awful experience, but it was a mistake that should never have happened. "I'm in no hurry to jump back into a relationship, but it looks great on you. When did you and Max get together?"

"A few months ago," Layla said, returning to the desk. "He finally gathered the nerve to tell me how he felt. Of course, true to Max form, it wasn't the most romantic revealing. He blurted it out one evening as he was closing, and all I could say was 'what took you so long?'" Layla chuckled as she arranged things on the desk.

"Well, better late than never," Lanie said. "I'm glad you two got it together. Will there be a wedding soon?"

"I don't know," Layla said with a shake of her head. "Maybe after another decade, but a wedding is happening soon."

"Oh yeah? Who's getting married?" Lanie wasn't a fan of gossip, but in a small town where everyone knew everybody, it was hard not to be curious.

"Presley Hays and Brandon Scott. Remember them?"

Lanie searched her memory. "Behind us in school, right?"

"Yep. Presley moved back about nine months ago, and Brandon came home early December to help his father out. I guess sparks rekindled, and the rest is history as they say."

Lanie longed for a love story like that. Having always been a hopeless romantic growing up, she had pined for her wedding day, probably so much that she had put expectations on her relationship with Denny that he would never have been able to fulfill. "Well, that's great," she said, swallowing her own disappointment and faking happiness for the couple. "I should run to the realtor soon, but I wanted to ask, is The Diner the best place for coffee or have we gotten anything better?"

Layla chuckled. "I'm a bit biased, but I think Max's coffee is fine. However, if you're looking for something other than black, Presley opened Sweet Treats across the way and makes a decent cup too."

"Thanks, I'll try it. I'm working for my father until something better comes along, but we should get together soon."

"You bet," Layla said, as the phone rang. She waved goodbye as she picked up the receiver. "Thank you for calling The Star Lake Inn, how can I help you?"

Lanie exited the way she had come and climbed

back in her car. Though she desperately wanted a cup of coffee, with no idea how long the house search would take, she figured she should hit the realtor first.

A petite blond woman was opening the office as Lanie pulled in. Since she didn't recognize the woman and the name of the building wasn't what she remembered, Lanie assumed she was newer to town.

After locking the car doors, Lanie dropped her keys in her pocket and pushed open the door to the realtor office.

"Hello," the woman said, greeting her as she walked in. "I just opened, but I'll be happy to help you in a minute. Would you like coffee?" She pointed to a Keurig and Lanie smiled, nodded, and walked to the table.

A silver metal tree-like apparatus sat next to the dispenser holding a variety of pods. Lanie grabbed a caramel mocha one and popped it in the coffee maker. When the coffee had filled, she held it to her nose, sniffing in the wonderful aroma before taking a sip. The warm beverage flowed down her throat, warming her from the inside out.

"Okay, I'm ready now," the woman said. "Have a seat." She pointed to the chairs across from the desk, and Lanie sat down in the one closest to her. "I'm Annie Goodman," she said, reaching her hand across the desk for a shake. "What can I do for you today?"

"I'm looking to rent a house. One or two bedrooms. Something in town if possible."

Annie's pink lips pursed as she turned to the computer on the right side of her desk. "Hmm, I rented the last two-bedroom house in town a few weeks ago, but let me see if there is a one bedroom available."

Lanie wasn't surprised at the lack of real estate. Few people moved to Star Lake unless they were moving back to be near family, like she was.

"Well, I have two. I'm sorry that's not much selection, but would you like to see them?

"Yes, please." Large selection or not, Lanie needed a place that wasn't her old room in her parent's house.

Annie led the way, flipping the open sign over so it now read 'be back soon.'

"Aren't you going to lock the front door?" Lanie asked.

"No need," Annie said. "There's nothing here to steal and besides, it's warmer in here than waiting outside if someone else comes by. Shall we take my car?"

Lanie nodded and climbed in the passenger side, curious how Annie could stay warm in her knee-length pencil skirt and heels. Though she wore a long-sleeved shirt, she hadn't even grabbed a coat.

The first stop was a small brown and tan cottage on Earl street. It appeared in good shape from the outside with a little garden area and a single car garage. The inside was also in decent shape. A beige carpet lined the floors, and the kitchen and bathroom boasted a neutral color scheme. Though the bedroom was a little smaller than she was looking for, Lanie liked that the house was close to work, which meant she could walk and save on gas.   The second house was a little bigger, but farther on the outskirts of town, and though it was a little cheaper, it didn't have the homey feel the first house had presented.

"Well, have you decided?" Annie asked as Lanie finished the tour of the second house.

"Yes, I like the first place. I'll be working at my dad's ice cream shop, and I like that I could walk to work."

Annie's eyes lit up. "Oh, Mr. Perkins? I love his triple chocolate brownie sundae."

Lanie smirked as she remembered the day she created that dessert. Donald Preston, a boy from a neighboring town, had decided she was too mousy and ordinary to continue dating. Crushed, she'd wandered into the shop, looking for something chocolatey to drown her sorrows in. She'd dumped in brownies, Oreos, and chocolate chips. Then she'd topped it with chocolate ice cream, whip cream, chocolate sauce, and a cherry on the top for good measure. The dessert hadn't healed her broken heart, but it had tasted delicious, and she'd named it the Triple Chocolate Brownie Sundae and added it to the menu. "Yep, that's my favorite dessert too. I named it when I was sixteen."

"That's so sweet that your father kept it all these years. I shouldn't frequent the shop as much as I do," Annie said, leaning in as if sharing a juicy secret, "but with no real night life and few men around, a girl's gotta do something for fun, you know?"

"What brought you out here then?" Lanie asked. She knew how boring her town could be.

"My uncle owned the realtor office before me, but he retired to Florida. Having no kids of his own, he called me up to see if I was interested. I was working in a competitive agency in Atlanta, so I thought owning an office might be a good change of pace, but I failed to realize just how small this town is."

"It grows on you though," Lanie said, "and the town puts on great festivals near the holidays."

"I'll look forward to that then," Annie said with a laugh. "Well, shall we head back and get your paperwork in order?"

Lanie nodded and a few minutes later they were pulling into the office parking lot again.

Azarius lay in the middle of his bed watching the black netting sway back and forth from the gentle breeze blowing in the window. There was a chill in the air, but he didn't feel it. He was too numb. The smell of her shampoo, some strawberry vanilla concoction, still lingered on his pillow, and when he closed his eyes, he could see her auburn hair splayed across his pillow. It had only been one night, but it was a night burned in his memory.

When she had finally responded to his text that she thought their night together had been a mistake, he had understood. After all, he knew her religion was important to her, and she had reacted emotionally to her divorce finalization - his own had been finalized for over a year - but when a second message had come in that she was leaving town, he'd retired to his room. Though he knew he cared for

Lanie, he hadn't expected her leaving to hit him so hard.

A knock sounded at his door, but he chose to ignore it, hoping his roommate would go away. Normally, Greg would never enter his room, but he hadn't spoken to him all day. Azarius had barely left his room for work, and as soon as he'd gotten home, he had retired up the stairs, not even flashing a wave or granting a mumble as he passed Greg.

"Az, you okay man?" The door swung in a few inches, and Greg's bearded face appeared in the small crack. "I've never seen you like this."

"I'm fine," Azarius said. He grabbed the remote and turned up the volume. Real Life's "Send Me An Angel" blared out of the big screen TV, reminding him of the first day he met her.

Azarius opened the glass door and stepped into the foyer of the radio station. A woman's voice echoed over the loudspeaker.

"That was Real Life's "Send Me an Angel," which was made famous by the movie The Wizard."

He looked around for the voice. An older woman manned a large desk in the middle of the room, but a phone was to her ear, so it wasn't her voice he had heard. To his left was a glass window, but an older gentleman stood in front of a mic. Azarius turned to his right, and his lips parted. Behind a similar glass window, a beautiful woman stood speaking into a mic.

"I always loved the beat in the middle. I know you can't see me jamming, but I have an air drum solo every time I play this song. Now I know why my mother never let take drum lessons."

The smile that stretched across her mouth lit up her whole face. She looked up, catching his eyes, and flashed another smile.

"I'm Lanie Wolffe, and you're listening to Mixx 98.6. Be sure to give me a call if there's something you want to hear. Duran Duran's "Come Undone" is coming up next, so don't go far."

The voice was replaced by the sound of commercials, and Azarius shook his head. He missed the angelic melody of the woman. She glanced his direction again, and seeing him still watching her, she raised her hand in a small wave. A playful smile resided on her lips, and she flashed a wink with her left eye.

Azarius returned the wave and then continued on to the desk. Whoever the redheaded beauty was, she was not the one he was supposed to be meeting, at least he didn't think she was.

The woman behind the desk hung up the phone and glanced up at him. "Can I help you?"

"Yes, ma'am. I'm Azarius Jacobson, and I'm here about the engineer position." He pulled his resume out of the satchel he was carrying and slid it across the counter to her.

"Ah, yes. Wait here, and I'll call Mr. Johnson."

"You are not fine. What is going on? Talk to me man." Greg still didn't dare to enter fully into the room. Thankfully, he'd known Azarius long enough to know that his room was his sacred space.

"I don't feel like talking right now."

"Alright, brother, but I'm here if you need me." Greg wasn't his brother, but they had been friends for the last few years and Greg had helped Azarius through some very tough times.

Azarius mumbled and rolled his face into the pillow that still held her smell. A minute later, the door clicked closed, and the darkness descended once more. Closing his eyes, Azarius replayed the last few months with her in his mind, ending with the night that ended it all.

The raucous night had been at her prompting. Perhaps he should have tried harder to tell her no; maybe he should have demanded they wait, or maybe it wasn't even the night itself. Maybe it was his evasiveness. He thought back to the many times she asked him to open up and mentally kicked himself. Would he ever get the chance to show her his true feelings?

CHAPTER 6

*L*anie sighed as she donned the pink apron with a smiling ice cream cone on it a few days later. This certainly wasn't how she had seen her life going, but it was a minor setback. Once she figured out what she wanted to do next, she could start saving and move on from here. At least she had managed to find a small house to rent, so she no longer had to live with her parents, even if she did have to work for them.

She pulled out her phone and checked the screen for the umpteenth time. Even though she had been the one who said they shouldn't see each other again, she had expected he would reach out to her, but her phone remained silent. Perhaps Greg had been wrong about his feelings for her.

The bell above the door jingled, and Lanie pocketed the phone, hoping her visitor hadn't caught her slacking off.

"Whatever you're hiding, you don't have to hide it from me," Layla said with a laugh.

"Hey, what are you doing here?"

"I came for the ice cream of course," Layla said, swinging her slim hips onto the barstool across from Lanie. "I took a dinner break with Max and thought I'd stop in to see you. You all settled in?"

"Mostly, I still have a few boxes to unpack. I know coming home was the right thing to do, but I have to admit it's kind of quiet and lonely in the evenings."

Layla's lips pulled into a knowing smile. "I understand that. Even when Max and I hang out, he isn't the biggest conversationalist."

Lanie smirked, remembering many of her evenings with Azarius. He wasn't much for conversing either, preferring to watch videos and engage in small talk when necessary. Still, there had been a comfort with him, an ease she hadn't felt with Denny in a long time, and somehow being near him had been enough, until she ruined it.

"What are you thinking about?" Layla asked, narrowing her eyes and leaning across the counter.

"Nothing. What do you mean?" Lanie grabbed a

rag and began wiping the counter, keeping her eyes away from Layla's penetrating gaze.

"You know what I mean. You were just thinking about something or should I say someone," Layla said with emphasis. "You got all moony faced."

Lanie sighed and stopped pretending to clean. "I was thinking about this man I left in Dallas.

"Denny?"

"No, not Denny." Layla's brow arched and Lanie knew there was no way she would drop the subject now.

"When Denny and I separated, I ran into an old friend I used to work with. We met years ago at the radio station - he was an engineer, though I don't remember him much from back then. He disappeared about the time I married Denny, but the day Denny left, I went to the old bar hangout and he was there. We started talking, realized we had a lot in common, and began hanging out."

Layla folded her hands and placed her chin on the top of them. "And?"

Lanie rolled her eyes. "It's not what you think. We watched eighties videos and made fun of them, but it was comfortable. Anyway, we began hanging out more often, once or twice a week."

"Don't you mean dating?" Layla asked.

A small snort escaped Lanie's lips. "I don't think you could call it dating. We didn't go anywhere together, just hung out at his house."

"That doesn't sound fun," Layla said slowly.

Lanie sighed. "It wasn't about what we did. It was just being together. We'd dance to old songs or watch old videos and sing. When he looked at me, I felt like he was seeing me, like he cared about my interests."

"Is he a good kisser?"

"What?" A blush spread across Lanie's cheeks, and she averted her eyes.

"You heard me. I refuse to believe you only watched old videos on television, so spill it."

Lanie bit the inside of her cheek, remembering the first time she and Azarius had kissed. While this kiss itself had been okay, it was the look in his eyes before their lips touched that had seared itself in her memory and kept her coming back for more. "Fine, yes, he's a good kisser, but he doesn't kiss much."

"What do you mean?" Layla leaned back and folded her arms across her chest.

"I don't know; it's weird. I love kissing, but he didn't initiate it much."

"Was that why it didn't last?"

Lanie shook her head. "No, while I would have preferred more, there was something about the way he looked at me that made the kissing or lack thereof not as important."

Layla leaned forward and splayed her hands across the counter. "Okay, what happened then?"

"It just didn't work out," Lanie said, skirting the question. "I think I was looking for more than he was, and I realized it would never work in the long run."

"Well, it's good you found out now," Layla said. "You know what you want now, so why mess around?"

Lanie nodded, glad that Layla wasn't pushing further. She was embarrassed she had let the last night happen, and she didn't feel like airing that laundry yet.

The overhead bell jingled again, and both women looked to the door. A man in a checkered shirt and drab brown coat entered. His hair was perfectly slicked down except for a cowlick in the back that resembled Alfalfa.

"Hello, Bert," Layla said, "What are you doing here?"

"Oh, hello, Layla, I wasn't expecting to see you here. I heard a familiar face was back in town, and I thought I'd come and say hello to Lanie. Hello, Lanie." He raised his hand in a wave.

Lanie pasted a smile on her face. "Hello, Bert."

"Why didn't you bring Amelia?" Layla asked.

A red blush spread across Bert's cheeks. "Oh, Amelia had to work late, but I'll probably bring her next time. Well, nice to see you again, Lanie." Bert executed an awkward bow before turning and scooting out the door.

"What was that about?" Lanie asked.

A small chuckle escaped Layla's mouth. "I'm pretty sure he was coming here to check you out. Though he has been seeing Amelia, I don't think it's as serious as he would like, and you are the new commodity in town. You're welcome."

It took a moment, but when Layla's meaning clarified in Lanie's head, she laughed as well. "You don't think he'd try to ask me out, do you?"

"I wouldn't put anything past Bert. I stopped trying to understand him years ago." Layla's dark locks bounced as she shook her head. "Well, I better get back to the inn."

"Wait, will you go to church with me on Sunday?"

Layla hesitated. "I don't know, Lanie. Church isn't really my thing."

"I know, but it's my first week back, and I wasn't very dedicated back in Dallas. I want to try to recommit, but I don't really remember everyone, and there are some new faces."

Layla looked unconvinced.

"Please, don't make me have to sit with my parents." Lanie knew she was begging, and while she was perfectly capable of sitting alone, the thought held no appeal.

"Alright," Layla said with a sigh. "I'll go with you this week, but don't get used to it."

Lanie smiled. If she could get Layla in the door, there was hope she could get her to see religion wasn't bad. Lanie had never pushed Layla, but she had always prayed for her and now that she was back in town, it seemed the perfect time to motivate her more closely.

It was dark when Lanie left the store that night. The air was still crisp and cold, and Lanie hunched her shoulders against the chill. Few people lined the streets as most of Star Lake retired indoors when the sun set, but a few shop owners were locking their doors or just setting home as she passed them.

"Well, well, well. I wondered when I would see you, Lanie Perkins."

Paula's unmistakable boisterous voice sounded behind her and Lanie turned, forcing a tight smile across her lips. It wasn't that she disliked Paula, but the woman had to be at the center of everything and was a hopeless gossip, not of the malicious kind usually, but Lanie had been hoping to avoid being the center of Paula's attention.

"I'm so sorry. I've been meaning to come and see you sooner, but you know how it gets before a recital." She flicked a scarf as red as her lipstick over her left shoulder. "We are working hard for the summer program, though it certainly doesn't feel like summer right now, does it? Will you be coming?"

Paula's question appeared innocent, but Lanie knew ulterior motives threaded her carefully chosen words.

"I don't know, Paula. It depends on if my father needs me to work the shop that night."

"Of course, but I wanted to let you know that boyfriends are not required. You don't have to be part of a couple to come."

Ah, there it was. The dig. Even though Paula had never married that Lanie knew of, she had long been obsessed with men and often resented those who were in relationships. She was probably getting some sick pleasure out of Lanie's divorce.

"I mean, I heard about your divorce." Paula leaned forward as she spoke, whispering the last word as if it were a dirty secret. "We're all sorry for you, dear, but don't let that keep you from enjoying the festivities of the town."

"Don't worry, Paula, I won't." Lanie wanted to add a snippy remark about Paula never having a man either, but she chose to be the bigger person and keep the thoughts in her head. "It was good to see you." Before Paula could continue, Lanie twirled around and continued her walk to Earl Street. She had certainly not missed this aspect of small town life.

The dark house elicited a sigh from her as she rummaged in her pocket for the keys. Not for the first time, she wondered if she should have stayed in Dallas. There she had Azarius and his roommate Greg, whom she had gotten to know the last few times she had stopped by. Perhaps she and Azarius could have discussed their mistake and started over, but then she remembered the frustrating nights she had spent wondering why he wouldn't share information with her and the days she had spent waiting for a message from him asking her to come over, only to never get it and have to ask him if he wanted to see her. No, if she had stayed she would have been settling again, just like she had with Denny. She wanted someone to want her, to fight for her attention, and to share his life with her - the good and the bad.

With a sigh, Lanie flicked on the living room light and shut the door behind her. She was not going to settle this time even though it was tempting. At least she had her books and her television shows to keep her company until the perfect man came along. She might never have a chance with Jensen Ackles but he would do until her Romeo arrived.

A zarius scowled as Greg changed the channel. "Hey, I was watching that."

"No, you weren't," Greg said, muting the television. "You were staring off into space, thinking about whatever you've been obsessing over lately, and I can't hear this song one more time. What does it even mean?"

"It means everything," Azarius said.

Greg shook his head. "Dude, sometimes your riddles are too hard to figure out. Is this about Lanie?"

The name sliced Azarius like a dagger, and his eyes darted to Greg, but he said nothing.

"Look, I wasn't going to pry, but she hasn't been around this week, and you've been in a dark place the last few days, and I know dark places, so I just figured they were connected. Tell me what happened."

Azarius shook his head and folded his arms. "It doesn't matter."

"Yeah, it does man. I can't keep seeing you like this, especially because I know how much she cared about you."

Azarius's eyes narrowed. "How do you know how she felt?"

Greg sighed. "Because she told me man. You remember that day you were helping my sister out, and you came home late?"

The evening flashed to the front of Azarius's mind. He had made plans with Lanie when Cheryl had called, wanting help in moving furniture to set up a surprise party for Greg that weekend. Thinking he would have time to help before his date with Lanie, he had agreed, but the traffic along with Cheryl's indecisiveness had led to him arriving home over an hour later than he planned. Lanie had waited, but she hadn't been too happy with him. "Yeah, I remember. What about it?"

"I never told you, but Lanie came in that night at eight. I had left the door unlocked, and I guess she thought maybe you fell asleep waiting for her, so she tried the lock and came in when it opened. Scared me half to death," he laughed, "because I was sitting in the kitchen in the dark nursing a headache. It was a day my depression hit hard, so I hadn't been sleeping much."

Azarius motioned for him to continue, trying to urge him to get to the meat of his story.

"She asked if I knew where you were, and I didn't at the time, but I told her she could wait for you. Anyway, we got to talking, and I asked her how serious she was because you know, I wanted to look out for you and avoid another Krista. She told me she could be serious if she knew you were serious."

"I was serious," Azarius said, leaning forward.

Greg held up his hand. "I know you were, but she didn't. She said she was confused by you; she wanted you to open up to her more, to show her you wanted her."

"I sent her that song."

"What song?" Greg asked, confused. "That Nine Inch Nails song you keep playing? That's hardly romantic."

"But I told her she means everything."

"Yeah, but then you never ask her over," Greg continued.

"I told her she was always welcome," Azarius protested.

"That's not the same thing," Greg said. "She wanted you to want her to come over. She wanted to know that you wanted her around and not just that you didn't mind if she were here."

"How do you know that?" Azarius asked. While Lanie had told him she wanted him to want her, it had always been through texts.

"Because we texted a few times after that night," Greg said. "I didn't tell you because I didn't want you to think I was trying to pick her up, but she was confused and looking for answers. I never said much to reassure her though because I didn't want to cross you. Is that why she stopped coming around?"

The words bounced around his head. He had been sure she left solely because of the incident, but maybe it had been a combination of factors. "She stopped coming around because she moved," Azarius said.

Greg blinked. "She moved?"

"Yeah, when she came last time, she was emotional because her divorce had been finalized. I was elated because it meant we could be together, but we let our guard slip and we," he shrugged, "you know."

"Was it bad?" Greg asked.

"No, it was amazing," Azarius said with a smile, "but I shouldn't have let it happen. I knew she didn't believe in intimacy outside of marriage, but I didn't stop it. The next day she texted that it had been a mistake and she wanted to step back. I was fine with that, but then I got a message that she was moving back to her hometown."

"You think it was just because you guys crossed the line?" Greg asked.

"I did, but after what you said, I'm wondering if I drove her away before that. Maybe the incident wouldn't have been that upsetting if I hadn't kept her at arm's length before that."

"So, what are you going to do?"

Azarius shrugged. "What can I do?"

Greg's head dropped forward as his brow arched. "What do you mean what can you do? You go and get her."

"She probably wouldn't come back anyway."

"That's not the point. Do you miss her?"

Azarius nodded.

"Do you love her?"

"I," Azarius opened his mouth and paused. Did

he love her? He enjoyed having her around, and he always felt better when she was in the room, but was that love? "I don't know," he said. "All I know is that everything feels more complete when she's here."

"Then you have to tell her," Greg said. "Where is her hometown?"

"I don't know, some small town. Sun City? Star Shore? Star Lake," Azarius said, snapping his fingers.

Greg whipped out his phone and tapped the screen. "Star Lake isn't far from here. You could take some time off and go woo her."

"I can't take time off. I just started this new job."

"Then go on the weekend, man, but don't let her get away. I know you are scared, but I think you guys are perfect for each other, and I know you are going to regret it if you don't at least tell her." Greg tossed the remote back to Azarius and headed up the stairs to his room.

Azarius held his finger over the volume button, but didn't press it. Maybe Greg was right. Could he open his heart again and let Lanie fully in? More importantly, could he live with himself if he didn't try? He definitely didn't like the way he had been feeling the last few days, but would it get better? His friends called him a gambler, but he was no longer sure which would be the bigger gamble.

CHAPTER 7

*L*anie's doorbell rang at nine am on the button. Layla stood on the other side, nervously brushing her slacks.

"You made it," Lanie said.

"I feel silly. Do I look alright?" Layla tucked a dark strand behind her ear, and Lanie smiled at the nervous gesture. Layla was normally so collected; it was funny to see her struggling.

"You look wonderful, and it's church, not a dinner engagement. We're there to worship and reflect, not win pageants."

"I'm sorry. I told you I was no good at this," Layla said.

"You'll be fine. Want to walk or drive?"

"Drive. I want to get it over with."

"It's not a death march you know," Lanie laughed, grabbing her jacket and Bible before stepping out and locking the door behind her.

"Maybe not for you. Religion was never big at my house."

"It shouldn't be about religion anyway. It's about a relationship with Jesus." Something Lanie had forgotten lately.

Layla shook her head as she climbed in the passenger seat. "I don't see the difference, but that's okay."

Lanie smiled and put the car in gear. The church was just a few minutes down the road, a small building with beautiful stained-glass windows.

"I thought it would be bigger," Layla said as she exited the car.

Lanie chuckled. "Star Lake is a small town; why would we need a bigger building?"

"I guess that's true," Layla agreed. "I just think of the churches on movies I suppose. They are always big and imposing."

"My church in Dallas was a lot bigger, but I rather like the smaller, homier feel."

"Welcome to Star Lake Church." An elderly woman in a long dress smiled and handed them a thin bulletin.

Lanie couldn't remember her name, but she was fairly certain this same woman had been a greeter ten years ago before she left for college. "Thank you," she said, scanning the bulletin as she led Layla inside.

The layout of the service hadn't changed much either, it seemed. There was still music to open with, a prayer time, the service, and then closing music. What had changed was the pastor's name. She didn't think it had been Tom when she left though she couldn't remember what it had been. Also, the sanctuary had been updated.

The red velvet pews had been removed and replaced with rows of grey chairs. Lanie assumed the change had come about to offer more versatility to the space.

A white screen now hung at the back of the stage as well for the words to be projected on and several more instruments filled the stage area. All Lanie remembered was a piano before she left, but now there was a drum set and at least two guitars as well.

The room was not yet full as she led Layla to a seat near the front; however, before they even sat down, they were approached by several elderly women.

"Lanie Perkins, is that you?" one woman with a

slightly blue tint to her hair asked. "I haven't seen you in ages. Are you home for good?"

"For now," Lanie said.

"We were so sorry to hear about your divorce," the other woman added, "but I bet your mother is so pleased to have you home."

"I'm sure she is," Lanie said with a tight smile. An awkward silence descended until finally the women pretended to see someone else to talk to and scurried away.

"Ugh, that is the one thing I didn't miss while I was gone," Lanie said to Layla. "I hate that everyone knows everything about you in small towns."

Layla nodded. "Definitely hard to keep secrets, that's for sure."

The musicians came out then and the worship began. Lanie enjoyed the familiar songs, and though her life was not where she wanted it to be, she felt a small measure of peace as the music flowed around her. The new pastor was a good speaker as well though Lanie was surprised by how young he seemed.

When the service ended, she turned to Layla. "Well, was it as bad as you thought it would be?"

With a slow shake of her head, Layla responded, "No, it was actually kind of nice. I might even consider coming back sometime."

Lanie smiled as a feeling of joy for her friend coursed through her. "Good, well how about some lunch? I'll treat you to one of Max's famous cheeseburgers."

Layla laughed as she stood and filed out of the row. "You do know I get my food for free now that we're dating, right?"

"Now that you're dating? I bet you never paid for food," Lanie teased.

"Yeah, I guess you're right."

The girls' laughter was cut short as Lanie's parents appeared in the exit doorway.

"Lanie, we're so glad to see you made it to church," her father said.

"Yes, Dad," Lanie said with a sigh. "Just because my marriage didn't work out doesn't mean I'm not still committed to Jesus. I plan to be here every week for as long as I'm in town."

"That's wonderful, Dear," her mother said. "Perhaps you could come over soon for dinner. We haven't seen you in nearly a week."

Lanie swallowed a sigh. She had enjoyed not being around her father every day, but she knew, living in town, her parents would want to see her more often. "I'll try to get out this week, Mother."

"Good, have a wonderful week, sweetheart."

Elaine drew Lanie in for a hug before turning away to greet a friend.

"Hurry, before anyone else stops us," Lanie whispered. The girls sped up their footsteps as they trotted out to the car.

"I guess I'm glad my folks don't live in town," Layla said, a teasing gleam in her eye.

"Yes, you should be very glad. On the other hand, it is nice having family around."

The two women piled into the car for the short trip to The Diner.

CHAPTER 8

"*D*o you want me to come with you?" Greg asked as he leaned against the doorframe and watched Azarius pack an overnight bag.

"Not this time," Azarius said, rolling a shirt and stuffing it in the duffel bag. It was a tactic he had perfected from his many deployments while in the Army. "I don't know if she'll even want to see me. I'd rather my humiliation happen in private if it's going to happen."

"She's not going to turn you away," Greg said. "I'm telling you, I think she really cares for you."

"We'll find out soon enough. At least Star Lake isn't too far away, so worst case I'll be out some gas and maybe a night's stay somewhere." Azarius ducked into the bathroom and grabbed his razor and deodorant.

"You have to stop thinking like that," Greg said when he came back into view. "Think positive for once in your life."

Azarius sighed. He knew Greg was right. His negativity was part of what had driven Lanie away in the first place, but he'd learned long ago it was effective in protecting his heart. Unfortunately, it also kept him from getting close to anyone, and now he'd finally met a woman he wanted to get close to. He pulled the string, closing the bag, and threw it over his shoulder.

"Okay, hold down the fort and wish me luck."

Greg stepped out of the way, so he could pass by. "You don't need luck if you just tell her the truth."

Azarius set his jaw and nodded. The truth. Hopefully, he would be able to do, but he'd been deflecting so long he wasn't sure he knew how to tell the truth any longer. He flicked his hand in a wave and headed down the stairs, grabbing his keys from the entry way table as he stepped out of the front door and pulled it shut behind him.

He opened the door to his lime green Mustang, tossing the duffel bag on the passenger seat before settling down in the black leather driver's seat. The leather molded to his body, providing a modicum of comfort to his anxiety-ridden heart.

Two hours later, he slowed the car as he entered the small town of Star Lake. The green sign had boasted less than five thousand residents, and the existence of a solitary street light enforced that idea. As he passed through the small downtown area, he realized he had no idea how to find Lanie, but surely in a place this small, he could just ask in one of the businesses and find her.

When the store fronts faded into residential houses, he turned the car around and headed back for the main corner. A diner on the corner looked well lit, so he chose that and pulled into a spot in front.

Though lighted, the diner was mostly empty. A stubbled man in a ball cap and a flannel shirt stood behind the counter, a younger man in a checkered shirt sat at the counter, and a large woman with big hair and red lips filled a table.

All eyes turned to him as he stepped through the door. Not unfriendly, the eyes were still wary, and the silence pressed down on him.

"Ahem, hello, I'm from out of town, but I'm hoping you can help me. I'm looking for Lanie Hall."

There was a moment of silence as the three

looked from one to the other. The woman spoke first. "I assume you mean Lanie Perkins who came back to town a few weeks ago."

Perkins? The name confused him until he remembered that must be her maiden name. She had been Lanie Hall for most of the time he had known her, and if she had changed it back after the divorce, she hadn't told him.

"Yes, I am sure that's who I mean. Can you tell me where I can find her?"

"Well, I don't know if we should be sharing that information," the flannel-clad man said, crossing his arms and leaning back against the counter.

"Oh, I don't see the harm, Max," the woman said. "He said he was her friend." The way the woman emphasized the word friend made Azarius slightly uncomfortable, but if she led him to Lanie, that was all that mattered. "Lanie is working down at Perkins Ice Cream Parlor. Across the street."

Azarius nodded; he remembered the sign from his first time through town. "Thank you." He turned to leave, but the woman's voice stopped him.

"Shouldn't you at least tell us your name?"

"It's Azarius, Azarius Jacobson." He tapped his forehead in a mock salute before turning and exiting the diner. The ice cream parlor was a stone's throw from the diner, so Azarius didn't bother driving.

As he approached the ice cream parlor, his heart sped up in his chest. He had no idea how she would receive his showing up in her hometown unannounced.

The bell jingled overhead as he pushed open the door. Lanie stood on the opposite end of the room near the cash register. Her face was focused downward as she spoke.

"Welcome to Mr. Perkins, what can I…?" Her voice trailed off as she looked up and saw him for the first time. "Azarius? What are you doing here?"

"Hi, Lanie. I needed to tell you some things."

He had hoped to see a smile or some sort of joy at seeing him again, but her face remained stoic. "Tell me? You rarely gave me a straight answer about anything, and then you didn't even try to stop me from leaving."

"I didn't know I was supposed to try to stop you from leaving. I thought giving you your space was what you wanted."

Her face softened slightly. "Fine. What's so important that you had to drive two hours to see me?"

Azarius sighed. "You aren't going to make this easy for me, are you?"

"No, I'm not," she said, leaning against the back wall as if trying to put as much space between them as possible. "I thought we were friends if not more after the last night, but I still don't even know when your birthday is."

He forced himself not to roll his eyes. Azarius should have just told her his birthday, but ignoring it was easier than telling most people why he didn't like birthdays. "I told you my birthday isn't a big deal. I didn't want you to make a big production of it because I'm terrible at reciprocating."

"I never said I had anything big planned. I just wanted you to share a part of your life with me. It's like you keep me at arms' reach most of the time. I wanted you to want me, but I always had to be the one calling or the one coming over. It's like you couldn't be bothered to contact me first."

Azarius thought back over the last few months and realized she was right. Other than the first few times they hung out, it had always been her asking to come over. Perhaps it had been his emotional wall to protect himself or perhaps he had just been being lazy, but he knew if he was going to have a chance with her, he needed to change that right now.

"You're right," he said, crossing the remaining distance until he was on the other side of the counter. "I can't apologize enough to you, but when you left, it made me realize how much I cared for you. I don't know if you can, but I'd like to give it another shot. I miss you, Lanie."

"I miss you too," she said, and the words lightened his heart, "but I don't know if it would be a good idea. I mean I live here now, at least for the time being, and I assume you'll still be in Dallas."

"I will, but we could spend weekends together until we figure it out. We could take turns driving, or to prove to you how serious I am, I'll drive every weekend."

"We can't let what happened, happen again," she said with a slight hesitation as if testing the waters.

"I'm okay with that," he said, leaning forward on the counter. "While that night was great, and I do look forward to a repeat performance someday, what I realized was that I felt complete just having you around, even if all we were doing was watching television, and I was miserable without you."

Lanie's hazel eyes bored into his soul. He resisted the urge to look away, to turn tail and run. He wanted her to see how serious he was even if her penetrating gaze made him squirm. "Will you let me in?" she asked.

And there it was. The one question he had hoped she wouldn't ask because he didn't know if he could. "I'll try. There's stuff in my past that has made me the way I am, but I really want to try, Lanie."

"I want to believe you, Azarius, I do, but I don't know. I don't know if my heart can take any more of this roller coaster of being up when I'm with you and down in the dumps when you don't call for days."

A tightening like a squeeze from a vice surrounded his heart. What if she said no? What was he going to do?

"I need some time," she continued. "Can you give me a week and let me think about it?"

It wasn't what he hoped to hear. He had hoped she would jump into his arms where he could smell the sweet scent of her shampoo, but he couldn't blame her for being protective of her heart. After all, it was why he was so guarded. "I'll give you as long as you need," he said.

Even though Lanie nodded, the gesture was like a dagger in his heart. "Well, I guess I'll be heading back then. Is it okay if I text you?" It was a cheap substitute to having her there, but it would be better than nothing.

For the first time since he had walked in, a smile touched her lips and almost reached her eyes. "Sure, I'd like that. I find myself checking my phone in hopes of a message from you."

"Me too," he said. Azarius wanted to walk around the counter and kiss her, hug her, or touch her in some way, but he felt he was already on shifty ground, so instead he sucked in his disappointment, flashed her a smile, and walked out of the small ice cream shop.

Lanie sagged against the counter as Azarius walked out the door. His showing up had been a complete surprise and a part of her had wanted to race around the counter into his arms, feel his lips on hers and his arms around her. She wanted to inhale the manly scent she couldn't seem to erase from her mind, but then she'd remembered him avoiding her questions. She'd remembered all the nights she'd checked her phone every five minutes hoping to hear from him only to be disappointed and had stopped herself.

To his credit, he had apologized, and his face had seemed earnest. Lanie had never considered him a player, but she wanted to be sure he meant it. She wasn't certain her heart could take much more of the roller coaster experience it had been on lately.

"Lord," she whispered softly, "please give me a sign. I'm so confused, and I could really use your help."

Less than an hour later, the overhead bell jingled, and Paula's large frame filled the doorway. Her eyes swept the empty room before she stepped inside and let the door close behind her.

"Where's your friend, dear? I thought he'd still be here."

"What friend?" Lanie asked, feigning ignorance. The last thing she needed was Paula in her business. If Paula knew, then the whole town would know shortly, including her father, and she couldn't imagine him approving of Azarius. Her father wasn't overtly racist, but he'd always discouraged her from dating black men stating that children of mixed marriages didn't fully belong in either the white world or the black world, a statement Lanie had never understood or agreed with. Plus, black or white, he wouldn't understand her jumping into a relationship so soon after her divorce from Denny.

"Why, your nice African American friend, Azarius. He stopped into The Diner looking for you.

I told him where to find you. He seemed a man on a mission."

"Oh, yes, he did," Lanie said. "He was returning something he had borrowed. Thank you for telling him where to find me." She hated lying, but Paula couldn't know the truth, at least not yet.

The lie wasn't convincing enough though. Paula pursed her lips as her left eyebrow inched up her forehead, but she let the topic drop. "Well, I'm happy to have helped. I hope you have a wonderful evening, Lanie."

"You too, Paula," Lanie called. When the door closed behind the large woman, Lanie sighed with relief. Her secret was safe for a little longer.

The next few days flew by for Lanie. She spent the mornings either unpacking or visiting with Layla at the inn. After a quick lunch, she would work her shift at the store and then head home or to her parent's house for dinner. She'd kept herself so busy that she hadn't had much time to think about Azarius's visit or maybe she was just avoiding thinking about it. Though Azarius sent her a text each night, he had never hounded her for an answer, which was good as Lanie still didn't have one.

As she tugged on her jeans for the day, she was forced to suck her stomach in more than usual. "Diet," she said aloud, checking her reflection in the mirror. "It's time to start that diet. And get some concealer," she added, noticing a few red splotches on her face.

Lanie leaned in for a closer look. She'd rarely had skin blemishes, even as a kid. While her weight had never been something to brag about, Lanie had always taken pride in her smooth skin, but today not only did she have a few red splotches, but a pimple had also erupted on her face.

"I better cut back on the greasy food, too," she said, though she couldn't remember the last greasy meal she'd had.

With a shake of her head, she turned off the bathroom light and headed out the door.

Layla was in the kitchen when Lanie arrived at the inn, a large plate of scrambled eggs in front of her.

"Ugh, what did you put in that?" Lanie asked, covering her nose. "That stinks."

"The same thing I always do," Layla said,

shoveling a forkful in her mouth. "Since when does it bother you?" she asked after swallowing her bite.

Lanie's stomach tilted and churned. "I don't know. Since today I guess. The smell is making me nauseated."

Layla's eyes narrowed and scanned Lanie's face. "You feel nauseated?"

"That's what I said."

"Anything else unusual?"

Wrinkles appeared on Lanie's face as she scrunched it in confusion. "Unusual? What do you mean? My pants are a little tight, and I have these crazy red spots on my face, but…" Lanie paused as the implication hit her.

"No," she said, sinking into the seat and shaking her head. "No, no, no. It couldn't be."

"Would you get back together with him if you are?" Layla asked.

"What?" Lanie asked. The fog in her mind clouded Layla's words.

"Denny. Would you get back together with him if you're pregnant?"

Lanie rubbed a hand across her face. "It wouldn't be Denny's. We separated months ago, and it was longer than that since we were intimate."

Layla's eyes widened. "Then whose baby would it be?"

A notch in the table garnered Lanie's attention, and she dropped her eyes as she chose her words. "My friend Azarius's- you know the one I told you about."

"Wait, the one who didn't want the same relationship you did?" Layla asked between bites.

"Yeah, that's the one."

"I thought you didn't want a relationship with him because of that."

"I didn't. I was actually planning to call it off the last night I went over, but my divorce papers came in that day, and even though I was expecting them, the news sort of hit me emotionally. I went to see Azarius, and we ended up sleeping together."

A low whistle escaped Layla's lips. "Is that why he came to town?"

A shrug of her shoulders showed Lanie's nonchalance. "He said he wanted to try again, that he realized how much he cared for me after I left."

"That's good though, right?"

"It would be if he weren't so secretive. I like him, but I don't know if I can trust him. He won't even tell me his birthday. Plus, my father would have a conniption fit."

"He won't tell you his birthday?" Layla asked. "Why not?"

Lanie shook her head. It was a question she still didn't have the answer to.

"Well, you can't worry about your father. He comes from a different generation, but I'm sure he would come around. What are you going to do though?"

Tears pricked the back of Lanie's eyes. "I guess I'm going to take a test to see for sure, and then… I don't know."

Layla reached across the table and squeezed Lanie's arm. "It will be okay."

F ear parched Lanie's throat as she entered the general store. Though she knew she needed to do this, it didn't make the process any easier.

"Welcome to Star Lake General, can I help you find anything?"

The voice belonged to a teenage girl with horn-rimmed glasses and a blonde ponytail. Lanie envied her carefree expression. Probably the most stressful thing in her life was finals and if the boy behind her in math class liked her. Lanie missed those days, but she didn't need the pity of a teenager.

"No, thank you, I'm good." Lanie grabbed a basket from the stack and headed to the far right of the small store. She might as well grab the few other things she needed.

A few bagged salads and some vegetables found their way into her basket, along with a tube of toothpaste. Then Lanie found herself staring at the pregnancy tests. Even in this small store, there were five different options. She grabbed one that claimed it held two tests and gave accurate early results. A few final items finished her trip, and she made her way to the front to pay.

The same perky blonde stepped to the register and began scanning her items. Though she said nothing as the pregnancy test glided over the scanner, Lanie felt the girl's eyes glance at her left hand. Pregnancy outside of marriage was prevalent in the current year, but Star Lake moved to its own time, and it was an anomaly here.

Lanie kept her eyes downcast as she paid the checker and scurried out of the door, the bag clasped to her chest like a life jacket in a storm.

Though tucked away in the bag, the small box grabbed her attention every few minutes on the drive home, and once she stepped inside her house, it was the first item she removed. She placed it on the bar and stared at it a moment. The simple white box held her future, and the thought of that sent Lanie's heart racing.

It took every ounce of strength for her to put away the other groceries before sneaking off to the bathroom with the accusatory white box. Once inside, Lanie locked the door, not knowing why as she lived alone but feeling it necessary.

The instructions were pretty straight forward. Either pee on the stick or catch some in a cup and put the stick in the cup. Not having brought a cup with her, Lanie chose option one, hoping it would be accurate.

Afterwards, she wiped off the stick and placed it on a few pieces of toilet paper. Then she washed her hands and sat back down on the toilet seat to wait the three minutes the test needed.

Conflicting emotions washed over her as she waited. On one hand, she found herself hoping it would be negative. She could put the night out of her mind and start fresh. Another part of her, smaller but not non-existent, wanted it to be positive. The desire to have a baby had been creeping in on her, and maybe if a child was involved, Azarius would be less secretive and settle down. But then there was her father, who would not only be upset she was pregnant out of wedlock but would have an issue with Azarius's skin color.

A peek at her watch revealed only a minute had passed, but Lanie couldn't take the suspense any longer. She sat up a little straighter and let her eyes wander over to the stick.

CHAPTER 9

*A*zarius lay on his bed nursing his wounded ego. When Lanie had asked for a week to think about their relationship, he had agreed because he didn't believe she would need that long. He knew she was interested in him, and he had believed his apology would smooth over any reservations she still held, but it was now Friday, and he still hadn't heard her decision. Though he sent her a text each night to let her know he was thinking about her, he had been careful not to ask the one question that was constantly on his mind.

The doorbell rang, but Azarius made no move to get it. Not only was Greg downstairs, but Azarius didn't care who was at the door. He wasn't expecting anyone, nor did he care to see anybody, but as the voices carried upstairs, his mood changed.

"I'm not sure that's a good idea," Greg said.

"It's important, Greg, and I won't take no for an answer," Lanie replied.

Azarius sat up and regarded his appearance. Baggy sweats covered his legs, and his oversized t-shirt sported a small stain in the middle of his chest, but there was little time to change. He whipped off the t-shirt and grabbed a clean one from his drawer, pulling it over his head as the sound of footsteps on the stairs reached his ears.

A knock sounded at the door, and he opened it, glad his hair was short and therefore always decent, though when he went out, he spent more time on it. Lanie stood on the other side with a tight smile on her face.

"Hi, Azarius," she sighed. "Do you have a minute?"

Curiosity piqued, he gestured her inside, closing the door after her. "It's good to see you," he said as she sat on the edge of his bed. His small room held no other place to sit, only a dresser and a stand for the television.

"Thanks," she said, biting her lip. Her shoulders rose and fell in a sigh. "I don't know how to say this, so I'm just going to come out with it." She reached into her pocket and pulled something out, holding it out to him.

As soon as he recognized the white stick, his heart dropped. No wonder confusion clouded her face. He took the piece of plastic and stared at the display. Two blue lines filled the two windows. Pregnant! Had it been anyone else, he would have asked if it were his. After all, he and Lanie had never had the "let's be exclusive" discussion, but Lanie was different, and he knew she had been with no one else.

"It was one time," he said as he sank down on the bed next to her.

"It only takes once, Azarius," she said with an eye roll.

"I know. I just didn't expect it is all. What do you want to do?"

"Do?" Frustration dripped from her words. "There's no option here, Azarius. I don't believe in abortion, so I guess I'm having a baby."

"Then I guess I'm having one too," he said, though the words scared him to death. Azarius wanted children; he loved his nieces and nephews and believed he would make a good father, but he hadn't expected to be one so soon. Living with Greg had been enough of an adjustment. Could he live with a woman again?

"Azarius, you don't have to do that," Lanie said. "I didn't tell you expecting you to be heavily involved, but I thought you should know."

As she had yet to look at him, Azarius grabbed Lanie's face and turned it to face his. "I promise to be there for you. I take my responsibilities seriously."

"But you hate having a roommate. What if you hate living with me? I'm not the neatest person," she stammered. "I throw my clothes on the floor and don't get me started on dishes."

His hands moved to her shoulders. "I know I said I liked living alone, but Greg has kind of grown on me, and you'll be the same. We can make it work, Lanie. I came to Star Lake, remember?"

"I know, but that was before this. You haven't met my father. Not only will he not be pleased about the baby, but," - she paused and dropped her eyes - "he's kind of racist."

Azarius squeezed her shoulders. He had lived through racism before. "Look, he's from a different generation. You aren't racist and that's all that matters. I'm not having a baby with your father."

A small laugh escaped Lanie's tight lips, but it didn't reach her eyes. Azarius hated that their union, which he remembered fondly, was now causing her pain.

"How are we going to make this work?" she said. Liquid pools resided in her eyes, creating a glossy look.

"One day at a time," he said and pulled her into his arms. The sweet smell of her hair eased his nerves, and he ran his hand in a caressing gesture up and down her arm.

"Thank you, Azarius," she said, looking up at him. "I don't think I could have done this if you had said you didn't want the baby."

"I told you that night I don't run from commitments and I would be there for you no matter what."

Her hand found his cheek, and as her glistening, hazel eyes stared into his, he leaned down and placed his lips upon hers. It had only been a few weeks, but he had missed the feeling of her soft lips, and as unplanned as it was, he was glad the baby had brought her back to him.

Hours later when Lanie had left, Azarius ventured downstairs. Greg was parked on the couch in his usual position in front of the television. He glanced up as Azarius entered the living room.

With a deft movement, Greg lowered the volume and sat up straighter. "So, what happened?"

Azarius sat on the opposite end of the couch. "It was heavy. She's pregnant."

Greg let out a low whistle. "What are you going to do?"

With a shrug and a sigh, Azarius answered, "I'm going to be a father. I gotta tell you though I am excited and scared to death at the same time."

"I think that's natural," Greg said. "You going to move there or is she coming back here?" His eyes widened, and he leaned forward. "Am I going to need to find a new place to live?"

"Not yet. For now, she is deciding to stay in Star Lake, and I have to stay here for work. It's not a perfect situation, but we'll trade weekends."

"Well, I know it's not the way you planned it, but at least it means she's giving you another chance."

Azarius nodded, thanking God for that. Though he wasn't as religious as Lanie, he did believe in God, but he wondered if that difference would cause problems for them later on. Now that she was gone, the doubt crept in, and he began to wonder about a lot of things. Could he really do this? What if he were an awful father? He hadn't had one growing up for most of his formative years. It had just been his mother and him for his first ten years until his mother died and he was adopted. His adopted father had been okay while he was around, but Azarius had no idea what kind of father he would be. For the first time in a long time, he found himself praying.

CHAPTER 10

*L*anie bit the inside of her cheek as she paced the floor. Azarius was supposed to be driving in to meet her parents for the first time, and they were planning to tell them about the baby, although Lanie thought going in for a root canal sounded more appealing.

She checked her watch for the hundredth time and sighed. Her heartburn had been on overdrive this morning, and she had barely slept. Conversations of how this might go played over and over in her head, but none felt right.

The crunch of tires on gravel grabbed her attention, and she smiled as Azarius's turbo Mustang pulled into her drive. Then she snorted as she thought of strapping a car seat in his tiny backseat. Would

Azarius give up his mustang? And what if he drove like a crazy man with the baby in the backseat?

Lanie shook her head, forcing the questions from her mind. They had months to plan all that out. Today she needed to focus on her parents and what she was going to say to them. A baby had not been her plan, but she had been delighted that Azarius was willing to help raise the baby, and she enjoyed the feel of his arms again.

His muscular frame stepped out of the car. The air had warmed again, and the bright colors of spring stood out against his dark skin. She opened the door before he reached it and raced into his arms. The masculine, woodsy smell of him washed over her, calming some of her overworked nerves.

"It's good to see you too," he said with a chuckle.

"I'm sorry. I didn't sleep well thinking about talking to my father, but having you here makes it a little better."

His large hand smoothed her hair. "No matter what happens with your father today, it will be okay. I'm not going anywhere."

Though his words sounded perfect, Lanie still had doubts. She wanted to believe he'd be there forever, but there was still so much she didn't know about his past, and he hadn't opened up about everything.

After a brief tour of her small house, they set out for her parents' place. Though a few miles away, they decided to walk so Lanie could show him the main part of town.

"How long has your family run the ice cream parlor?" he asked when they passed it.

"As long as I can remember," she laughed. "My father's grandfather started it and my father has always wanted me to take it over. I don't know that it's in my blood though."

The door to The Diner opened as they approached, and Lanie sighed. Paula was hurrying their direction with a large smile on her face and an eagerness for gossip.

"Lanie, I see your friend has returned. Did he forget something again?" Her eyes dropped to their clasped hands. "Or is there more to the story?"

"Paula, this is my," Lanie paused. What did she call him? Her boyfriend? Her friend? They still hadn't finalized that discussion.

"Boyfriend," Azarius said, reaching out his right hand to shake Paula's. "I believe we've partially met, though I don't remember catching your name."

"I'm Paula Monroe. Delighted to officially meet you, Azarius. Will we be seeing more of you then?"

"I'm sure you will," he said. "Now if you'll pardon us, we have an appointment we must keep."

Paula's head snapped back in slight surprise, but as Azarius's tone had been nothing but respectful, she could say nothing. "Of course. Well, till next time then."

"You handled her so well," Lanie said, surprise threading her voice.

Azarius chuckled. "I met a lot of people like her in the Army. I learned very quickly how to be polite but distant."

"You'll have to teach me that skill," Lanie said with a smile.

"I'll be happy to teach you that and a lot more." Azarius squeezed her hand and returned the smile.

Her parents' house loomed in front of them before she was ready. As her heartbeat accelerated, sweat broke out on her palms and Azarius looked down at her.

"Sorry," she smiled up at him. "I just have a bad feeling this isn't going to go well."

Lanie led the way up the stairs and squared her shoulders before ringing the bell.

The door opened to reveal a smiling Elaine, but her smile faltered when she noticed Azarius. "I see you've brought a friend. Hello, I'm Elaine." She stuck out her hand and Azarius shook it in return.

"Nice to meet you ma'am. I'm Azarius."

"Hi Mom, Is Dad here too?"

Elaine's eyebrows rose on her head, but she nodded and stepped back, opening the door wider. "Yes, he is. Come on inside."

Lanie flashed a tight smile at Azarius before stepping into the entrance. The feeling of doom descended on her shoulders as they entered the family room where her father sat.

"Bob," her mother said, grabbing his attention. "Lanie's here with a friend."

Her father looked up and turned off the television.

"Hi, Dad," Lanie said. "Can we have a few minutes of your time?"

Her mother and father exchanged concerned glances, but Elaine pointed to the couch. Lanie took a deep breath and sat on the edge. Azarius followed suit and sat next to her. He folded his hands into his lap as if unsure where else to put them.

Lanie cleared her throat. "Dad, this is my boyfriend, Azarius." She glanced to him, and he nodded, encouraging her to continue.

"Boyfriend?" Bob said, leaning forward in his

chair. Lanie did not miss the disapproval in his voice. "That's a bit quick, don't you think?"

Lanie forced herself to take another deep breath before continuing. "We began hanging out several months ago when Denny and I separated, Dad, but we just started dating."

Bob's eyes narrowed as his arms crossed. "What does hanging out involve these days?"

"Not what you think, Dad." Lanie shook her head, trying to prepare herself for the worst. She dropped her eyes to her lap, unable to meet her father's eyes as she revealed the next part. "But we did have one night where we let things go too far."

Nothing but stony silence from her parents. Azarius squeezed her hand in silent encouragement. Lanie shot him a grateful smile and then looked back at her parents.

"Mom, Dad, I'm pregnant."

Silence fell like a blanket of snow. Elaine's eyes were wide saucers; her hand covered her mouth. Bob's eyes were daggers of ice, and the set of his jaw created a stony exterior. After a long moment, his eyes switched to Azarius.

"What are your plans regarding this baby?"

Azarius shifted in his seat. "I plan to be there, Sir.

I don't run from commitments. I already told Lanie that I want to be in the baby's life."

"In the baby's life?" Bob roared, leaning forward. "What does that mean? You'll do weekend visits? Send the child a card on holidays? Or do you plan to step up, be a man, and marry my daughter?"

"Marry?" The word came out strangled and slightly squeaky from Azarius's mouth, not a surprise to Lanie. If the man didn't like having a roommate, why would he want a wife? "We haven't really discussed that, Sir."

"Well, then it's probably high time you did," Bob said.

"Dad, we're adults. You can't force us to marry," Lanie said, trying to control the anger building up inside her.

"No, I can't force you to marry, but I can strongly recommend it. Children need both of their parents in their life, and occasional visits will not be enough. It's important for children to have a strong man in their life."

"It's also important they have two loving parents in their life, even if they don't live together. We told you as a courtesy, not so you could lay demands on us. Azarius and I will figure it out." Lanie bolted up from the couch and turned back to Azarius, her hand outstretched. "Let's go, Azarius."

His deep brown eyes regarded her before glancing to her parents and then back. He stood, though his posture displayed his continued uncertainty.

"Lanie," Elaine began.

"No, Mom," Lanie said, cutting her off. "I hope you guys will be a part of the baby's life, but you will have to be accepting of whatever we decide to do. I know two parents are important for a child, but not if they fight all the time or hate each other. I'm not saying that will happen, but if you force us into a marriage we aren't ready for, then it might."

"If you aren't ready for marriage, you shouldn't have been sleeping together," Bob said in a soft voice.

Lanie knew he was right, but her indignation wanted the last word. "We made a mistake Dad. I know you can't understand that living in the perfection you do, but we did, and we are trying to make it right the best way we know how." Lanie grabbed Azarius's hand and pulled him out of the room and out of the house. She didn't stop until the outside breeze smacked her in the face.

"Lanie, stop," Azarius said, halting his feet and forcing her to stop as well.

She turned to him, blinking back the tears that threatened to spill over her lids.

"Maybe your dad is right," he continued. "I grew up without a father, and it affected me. It probably is part of the reason I like living alone, but I don't want my baby... our baby to grow up like that, so... maybe we should think about getting married."

A sad combination of a snort and a laugh tumbled out of Lanie's mouth. "That's a heck of a proposal, Azarius. Just like I always dreamed."

His brows furrowed together and he dropped her hand to place both arms around her. "I know it's not, Lanie, and one day I'll make it up to you. I messed up, but I don't want to keep messing up."

Lanie blinked as she tried to process his words. "What are you saying, Azarius?"

"I'm saying let's get married. Let's elope and show your father we're serious."

"Elope?" Confusion clouded Lanie's mind, and she struggled to clear a path. "But what about our friends? Our family?"

"We can have another ceremony later and invite everyone. Let me at least look into it. Lanie, we're having a baby together. I want you as my wife."

Lanie wanted to say yes, but the pervading feeling that he was suggesting marriage solely because of the baby wouldn't leave her. She already had one failed marriage; she didn't want another. The memory of the night Denny moved out popped into her brain. She had spent hours online researching divorce, shocked by what she had found. The statistics on first marriages lasting was only about fifty percent and that number dropped to thirty three percent for second marriages. Lanie had no idea how long second marriages that occurred only because of an impending child lasted, but she feared the statistic was not a good one.

"Tell me your birthday," she said, throwing it out as a challenge. If he avoided the question like he had every other time, she would have her answer. They would never be able to make a marriage last, but if he....

"October 15th," he said without hesitation. His eyes fixed on hers, and she found her resolve melting in their chocolaty depths.

"Let me think about it, Azarius. I know you mean well, but there is still so much I don't know about you, that we don't know about each other. What if we get married and hate each other? That wouldn't be any better for the baby."

His eyes remained locked on hers, searching her soul. "Okay, take however long you need, but know that I don't run away from obligations, and whatever it takes, I will make it work."

Oh, how good his words sounded, and he had given up his birthday, but was it the start of something new or simply because he'd been backed against a wall? She needed time to think, to process, to be sure - if such a thing existed.

Knowing he needed some sort of response, she nodded and hugged him, savoring the security of his arms if only for a moment, before heading back towards her house.

L anie wandered aimlessly around her house that night. Azarius had stayed another few hours, and they'd cuddled on the couch and watched a movie, but Lanie's mind had been elsewhere.

Even now, in the stillness of her house, she couldn't get her mind to stop. Scenario after scenario played through her mind. Maybe a marriage could work. He could move here, or she could move back to Dallas with him, but did she want to move back? Though returning to Star Lake had never been in her plans, there was something about the small-town atmosphere she liked, and she'd enjoyed reconnecting with Layla.

Her eyes fell on her Bible. In the commotion of the last few days, she hadn't been reading on a daily basis. She picked up the black leather-bound book and held it to her chest. "Lord, I know we didn't do things right. I understand now why you wanted intimacy to belong in a marriage and not outside of it, but we want to do better. We want what's best for this child. Please show me what I should do."

Lanie let the silence cover her, and she listened for that still small voice. The one she could only hear when she was focused and willing to listen.

CHAPTER 11

"How did meeting the parents go?" Greg asked as Azarius returned that evening.

He fell into the oversized grey chair and collected his thoughts before answering. "I haven't met a lot of parents in my time, but that was definitely the worst experience. Her father hates me; I have no idea if he will even accept this baby. Her mother seemed nice, but we didn't chat for long. Oh yeah, and I asked Lanie to elope."

"What?" The TV picture faded to black, and Greg turned his full attention to Azarius. "You did what?"

Azarius ran his hands over his face. "It just slipped out. Her father was asking if I was going to marry her, and the very word felt like a noose you know? But then Lanie stormed out of the house. I could tell she was upset, and I thought maybe we should get married, and the words just slipped out."

"What did Lanie say?"

With a sigh, Azarius leaned back and shook his head. "She didn't jump on the idea. She told me it was an awful proposal, and it was. I keep messing everything up."

"Yeah, I can't say that was a great proposal, and my sister said women live for that day, but she ought to give you points for trying."

"I don't know. Maybe I'm not cut out to be married. Maybe Krista was a warning and this botched proposal is another sign."

]"Don't say that, man. I know what happened with Krista was hard, but Lanie isn't Krista. And you want to be a father. You tell me that every time you come back from your sister's house. You're ready, even if you don't think you are."

Azarius sat forward and dropped his hands. "You're right. I do want to be a father, and I'm excited about this baby. I'll just have to figure out a way to make everything else work."

After dinner that evening, Azarius lay in his bed

staring up at the black netting. His life felt out of control, and he wondered if this was why Lanie prayed. Did she find comfort in speaking to God?

Though he felt foolish, he opened his mouth and let the words fall out. "God, I don't know if you know who I am or even if you listen to people who haven't been following you, but I've messed up, and I'm hoping you can help me right things. I didn't have a father growing up, but I want to be one to this child. Help me to know what to do for the baby and for Lanie."

He waited, wanting some audible voice to reassure him, but nothing came. With a sigh, he rolled over on his bed and closed his eyes. Maybe something would come to him in the middle of the night.

No epiphany awaited him in the morning when he awoke, but a message from Lanie blinked on his phone.

-I thought about your offer. Let's do it. I'll be there later today.-

Azarius shook his head, wondering what had changed her mind. Deciding he didn't care, he showered and dressed before heading downstairs.

Sunday was his favorite day, not because he went

to church - he honestly couldn't remember the last time he had been - but because it was a day he could rest and not have to worry about work. He liked his job, but the late hours sometimes took a toll on him, and Sundays he claimed entirely for himself. He didn't even go to the gym on Sundays.

The downstairs was still dark and quiet as he made his way down the narrow steps. Greg usually slept in until mid-morning, so Azarius often had the mornings to himself. Not much of a coffee drinker, he headed straight for the griddle. Pancakes had always been what his mother had made when she had time in the mornings, and he had an affinity for them, but the weekends were the only days he had time to make them.

As he pulled out the large ceramic mixing bowl with a pouring spout, he remembered the last time his mother had made pancakes for him. At only ten, he'd had no idea how sick she was, and she had hidden most of her symptoms well. She'd made the pancakes extra special that day with chocolate chips for his birthday, and they had laughed and told jokes as they ate.

The next morning, he had awoken to a silent house and gone in search of his mother. It wasn't like her to let him sleep past school time. He had found her still and silent in her bed, and thinking her asleep, he had tried in vain to wake her. When she wouldn't rouse, he had climbed in bed next to her and cried until his tears ran dry.

The next-door neighbor found him like that a few hours later and gently led him out of the room and to her house. Years later he discovered she had been checking on his mother every day at eleven am for months. She knew to come over when the phone wasn't answered that day, though he had no memory of it even ringing.

It was only then he understood the cancer his mother had been battling. Not having the money to afford expensive treatments and with a less than stellar chance of living even with the treatments, she had opted to just take medicine to cope with the pain and spend her final days at home with him.

After that, he had been placed into foster care for a time until he met Mary. Mary was a spirited white woman recently married and ready to take on the world. Her marriage hadn't lasted, but the adoption had and though it had been strange growing up in a white world at first, Azarius had come to appreciate it. Now he had an insight into both cultures that helped him view the world in a different light. Perhaps if more people had his insight, there would be less racial hatred. And Mary was still his best friend and confidant. He told her everything. In fact, he needed to call her this morning and tell her about Lanie.

She already knew a little about Lanie as he had mentioned her the last time they spoke, but that was before the fateful night and definitely before the news of the baby.

He turned his attention to the mixing of the pancake batter, determined to call his mother after breakfast.

The smell of the pancakes woke Greg from his slumber, and he padded down the stairs rubbing sleep from his eyes. Lean and lanky, his baggy sweatpants barely hung on his hips and his loose shirt engulfed his frame. Short spikes of blond hair stuck up all over his head.

"You cooking?" he asked as he stumbled over to the coffee maker and grabbed the pot.

"Yep, you want some?" Azarius flipped the pancakes with a deft motion, keeping the circular shape.

"Of course, but not until I get some coffee. I still don't understand how you function without it." Greg filled the pot with water and poured it into the coffee maker and then shuffled to the cupboard for the coffee grounds. A few minutes later the sound of coffee dripping into the glass pot joined the sizzling sound of the pancakes.

Azarius turned the stove off, loaded the pancakes up on a plate, and brought it to the small table. He had to shove some papers to the far back as the table seemed to be the catchall place for all the bills and random papers throughout the week.

As he returned to the kitchen for plates, butter, and syrup, Greg sat at the table with a steaming mug.

"So, Lanie's coming over later," Azarius said as he placed a plate in front of Greg. "She agreed to elope, so I'm assuming she'll stay tonight so we can go tomorrow."

"That's good, right?" Greg asked as he stabbed a pancake and dropped it on the plate. "Where are you going to go? The court house?"

"I don't know. That seems so plain, and I already ruined the proposal for her. I'd like to do something nicer." He speared his own pancake and scooped out a pat of butter.

"You know, I heard someone at work talking about this bed-and-breakfast that does elopements. They have different packages you can choose from. You want me to find out more about it?"

Azarius nodded as he finished chewing. "Yeah,

that would be great. It would be good to do something special for her."

They finished the rest of breakfast in silence, and then while Greg retired to his second home, the living room couch, Azarius cleaned the table and put the dishes in the sink for later. Then he headed back upstairs to call his mother.

The phone rang only twice before his mother's voice came through. "Azarius! How are you, son?"

"I'm good, Mother," he said as he paced his small room, "but I have some news."

"Oh, yeah? About work?"

Azarius shook his head before remembering his mother couldn't see him. "No, work is fine." He adjusted the row of sunglasses on his dresser. "I um got a girl pregnant."

"Oh, Azarius," she sighed. "Do you love her at least?"

"I think I do, Mother. She completes me though I didn't realize it until she left."

"Wait? She left?"

"She did." He sat on the edge of the bed. "Lanie's pretty religious, and I think she regretted our night together."

"So where does that leave you two?"

"When she told me about the baby, I told her I

wanted to be a part of his or her life." Azarius grabbed the pillow with her lingering scent and held it in his lap. "I met her parents. They weren't exactly pleased."

"Well, it isn't the way I would have wanted it to happen for you either, but sometimes life doesn't turn out the way we hoped. I assume though you will be involved."

"Of course. I asked her to elope."

His mother whistled on the other end. "That's a big step. Are you sure? What about the religious difference? Don't you think that will cause problems?"

"Actually, Mom, I think there might be something to her relationship with God. I've found myself praying the last few days, and while I haven't heard an audible answer, I feel different."

"Well, if it makes you happy, I'll support you. So, tell me about this girl who managed to snag your heart."

Azarius smiled as he began discussing Lanie's finer points. "She was in radio when I met her, though she recently got out of that for the time being, but she has the most beautiful voice and smile. Whenever I'm feeling down, all she has to do is smile at me and everything just seems better."

"She sounds lovely, and I can't wait to meet her. And Azarius... I applaud you taking responsibility for your actions. Your mama would have been proud."

Tears pricked his eyes at the mention of his mama, who would never get to meet Lanie. However, maybe she was up in heaven looking down on him. While Azarius wasn't sure of her religious status, he did remember going to church with her on occasion and she had been the one who told him about God in the first place, so perhaps she had been a believer.

"Thanks Mom. I'm sure you'll get to meet her and your grandchild soon."

Azarius smiled as he ended the call. His mother might not be typical, but he loved the fact that she always supported him, and somehow, he knew that when they met, Lanie and his mother would get along well.

Lanie's stomach knotted as she pulled up to Azarius's apartment. Was she really going to go through with this? Even though she knew Texas had a seventy-two-hour waiting list - she'd researched it extensively the last few days - she was here to get the ball rolling as both parties had to be present to sign for the marriage certificate.

She had never expected to be eloping, but she'd had the big wedding once already and it hadn't turned out as planned. Maybe eloping wouldn't be bad, and at least it would keep the stares she feared from coming. Even though it was a quick marriage, at least she would be married when she started to show. Lanie just hoped her parents would forgive her one day.

Grabbing her overnight bag from the passenger seat, she exited the car, took a deep breath, and locked the door. She hadn't planned on staying with Azarius again until after they were married, but they would need to hit the courthouse early tomorrow for her to get back to work in time, and money was still tight.

The chime of the doorbell echoed and fell silent. Then footsteps sounded, and the door opened. Greg smiled at her from the other side.

"Hey, Lanie, long time no see."

Lanie returned the smile. Though they had only had the one heart to heart session, they had spoken by text a few other times and Lanie considered Greg a friend. "I know. I'm sorry." She shrugged. "Things got complicated."

"Well, at least you know he's serious now."

"Yeah, I guess. He upstairs?"

Greg nodded and motioned up the stairs. Lanie leaned in for a quick hug before tackling the ten short steps to the second floor.

Azarius's door was closed, but that wasn't unusual. He didn't like people in his room most days, but he had given her the green light to enter whenever.

The room was barely lit as she entered. Only the glow from the television that seem to constantly play eighties videos lit the room. Azarius looked up from the far side of the bed where he was packing a bag.

"Hi, you ready?"

Lanie blinked in confusion. "Ready? Ready for what?"

A slow smile spread across Azarius's handsome features. "It's a surprise. Did you bring a dress?"

"No, I didn't figure I'd need one to go to city hall. You do know we can't get married for another three days…"

"Oh, but we can." He closed the bag and came around the bed to grab her hands, lacing his fingers through hers. "Greg found a bed-and-breakfast in Oklahoma that performs ceremonies with no wait."

"What?" Though he was speaking English, Lanie couldn't comprehend the words.

"We can get married tonight. We'll even stop at a dress shop on the way, and I'll buy you a dress. It will be my gift to you."

"Tonight?"

"Yes, tonight. Say you will, Lanie. It's only a four-hour drive."

Lanie opened her mouth to answer, but words failed her. She had accepted the idea of being married again next weekend, but tonight? Azarius's chocolate brown eyes pulled her in, and she nodded. "Okay, let's do it."

A large smile broke out on his face, and he grabbed her face and pulled her in for a quick kiss. "Great. Do you have your divorce papers?"

"Yes, they're in my bag," Lanie said, patting the overnight bag.

"Good, mine too."

Lanie blinked at him. "Wait, you were married before?"

Azarius nodded. "It was finalized a year ago, but we had been separated years before that."

Another seed of doubt sprouted in Lanie's mind. What else was she going to find out about him? "How did I never know you were married?"

"Because I never told you. I don't talk about it much."

"But, don't you think that was important? How long were you married?"

"Five years, but we only lived together for three. Krista is partly why I'm so guarded about relationships." Azarius sat on the bed and patted the spot beside him. "Sit. I'll tell you about her. I can see you are curious and I don't want to start our marriage with this hanging over our heads. I promised to try to be more open, so I might as well start with this."

Lanie dropped her bag on the floor and sat down next to Azarius. He shifted slightly to face her and grabbed her hands.

"I don't know if I ever told you, but I liked you from the moment I saw you. I wanted to ask you out at the radio station, but before I got the nerve, you announced your engagement to Denny. It's stupid, but I kept hoping you would break it off, but when you got married, I had to leave."

"You left because of me?" Lanie had never known he had feelings for her back then, though he had said a few statements that had made her think he had.

Azarius nodded. "I was blindsided by your engagement, and I wanted you to be happy, but I couldn't stick around to watch it. It hurt too much, you know?"

Lanie pursed her lips together and nodded for him to continue. This was the most he had ever shared about his past.

"I took a remote tour after that. Remember when I told you I re-enlisted?"

She nodded.

"Well, on that tour I met Krista. She was a nurse, and I met her after spraining my ankle one day. We married over there, but Krista's deployment ended before mine. When I got back, things had changed, but I couldn't figure out why. At first, I thought it was that our interests weren't similar enough. It turned out the Army was about all we had in common, but a year later, I found out she was having an affair."

"Oh, Azarius, I'm so sorry," Lanie said.

Azarius shrugged his broad shoulders. "We tried counseling, and for a while I thought it was better, but then she took another deployment, and a fellow soldier sent me pictures of her and a new man over there. I filed for divorce after that, but she fought it for a time for whatever reason. She finally agreed a year ago. So there you go. That's the condensed version of why I'm guarded."

Lanie smiled and squeezed his hands. For the first

time, she felt confidence in their relationship. "I'm so glad you told me, though I wish you had told me sooner."

He nodded as a playful smile tugged the right side of his mouth up. "I know. I'm going to work on not hiding so much, but I'll need your help. Think you're up for the task?"

"Well, I guess I have to be," Lanie laughed. "Since we plan on getting married."

"Speaking of which," he said, "we should be going before the place closes. You ready?"

"Ready as I'll ever be," she smiled.

Azarius stood first, helping her up and then grabbed his bag from the bed. Lanie rescued hers from the floor and the two made their way down the stairs.

"Heading out?" Greg asked from the couch.

"Yep, thank you for the info, man."

Azarius extended his hand, but Greg stood and pulled him into a hug. Then he turned to Lanie. "I guess the next time I see you, you'll be Lanie Jacobson," he said, pulling her into a hug as well.

"Lanie Jacobson," Azarius chuckled. "Sounds like an author's name."

Lanie rolled the name around in her head and

decided she liked the sound of it. "Wish us luck," she smiled.

"You don't need it," Greg said. "You two were made for each other."

Azarius wrapped his arm around Lanie and pulled her close. "I agree."

Five hours later, Azarius pulled into the driveway of a large two story yellow house with white shutters. 'Forever Yours Bed and Breakfast' was scrolled across a sign that hung over the door and though there weren't many trees, the front of the house was landscaped beautifully.

Lanie sucked in a breath and turned to Azarius. "This is much nicer than a courthouse."

"I'm glad you like it. Shall we see what they offer?"

Lanie nodded and unbuckled her seatbelt. In the backseat, an elegant cream dress lay across Azarius's garment bag. She grabbed the dress and her overnight bag as he pulled out his suit and duffel bag. With fingers laced together, they walked up the cement walkway to the front door.

Before the chime inside had finished sounding, the white door swung open. An elderly woman with grey streaks in her dark hair stood on the other side. Her friendly smile soothed the last few raw nerves Lanie had.

"Welcome to Forever Yours," she said, clasping her hands in front of her. "I'm Stella White. Are you here to get married?"

"What gave it away?" Azarius asked.

The woman laughed a deep, hearty laugh and winked at Lanie. "You've got yourself a keeper here. I can tell. Well, come on inside and decide which package you'd like."

Stella stepped back and opened the door wide enough for Azarius and Lanie to step through. The white wall paper with gold striping grabbed Lanie's attention as they followed the woman to an ornate desk.

"Here we are. We offer five different packages, though if you want to get married tonight, you'll have to choose one of the pre-made cakes we have. Do you have guests?" Stella asked, looking past them as if she expected a crowd to enter at any moment.

"No, it's just us," Azarius said. "We plan to have a party back where we live later."

"Oh, well in that case, you probably only need to look at package one and two. The main difference is that package two includes a night stay in our honeymoon suite."

Azarius glanced Lanie's direction, and she felt the heat flood her face. "It would be a late drive back," she said.

"We'll take package two then," Azarius said to Stella.

"Wonderful."

As Azarius took care of the bill, Lanie wandered around the room. It was decorated with Victorian touches from the wallpaper to the settees. Along one wall rows and rows of frames hung in even spaces. Lanie leaned in closer and realized they were pictures of couples who had been married here. Underneath each one was the date they were married, but Lanie wondered how many were still together.

"If you'll come with me, I'll show you where you can change," Stella said, breaking into Lanie's thoughts.

Lanie nodded and followed the woman down a hall carpeted in a soft rose color to a white door with 'Bride' stenciled across the top in black. Across the hall was a similar door marked 'Groom.' With a final smile at Azarius, Lanie opened the door to her room and shut it behind her.

The room contained another settee, a full-length

mirror, a small vanity and stool, and a clothes rack. Lanie hung the dress and tossed her bag on the settee, then rifled through it for her makeup bag and brush.

As she brushed her hair out in front of the mirror, the nerves started again. In less than an hour, she would be Lanie Jacobson and the thought both thrilled and terrified her.

CHAPTER 12

*A*zarius hung the garment bag on the rack in his room and unzipped it. Though it wasn't a full suit, he had a dark suit coat and pants he had acquired years ago for a wedding or something. He didn't own a white button down shirt, but the pale blue one he had brought would suffice.

He peeled off his current shirt and flexed in the mirror. His arms were looking buff, but he'd need to do some more work on his chest to look his best for Lanie, though she hadn't complained last time.

Azarius grabbed the blue shirt off the hangar and poked his arms through. Thankfully, the buttons didn't stretch, though he wasn't sure he could have buttoned the one around his neck if he'd had to, but as he didn't have a tie that wasn't a problem, so he flipped the collar to make it lay just right.

The pants and the coat added the final touches, and he smiled at his reflection in the mirror. He hadn't been sure he would ever remarry, but he was looking forward to this union with Lanie and the prospect of being a father, even if it wasn't the way he planned it.

Azarius ran his hands down his sleeves one more time for good measure and then grabbed his divorce papers from his bag, tucking them in his suit coat pocket. Then he opened the door to the hall and peeked out. The door across the way was still closed, but Stella stood down the hall talking to an older man with a balding hairline.

"Oh, Azarius," Stella said as he approached, "I'd like you to meet John. He's our Justice of the Peace who will be performing the ceremony."

"Nice to meet you, Azarius," John said, sticking out his hand. He had a kind face underneath his bushy eyebrows which seemed out of place with his lack of hair. "Shall we get the paperwork started and Stella can wait for Lanie?"

Azarius nodded and followed John down the hallway to a small office. John crossed behind the desk and picked up a white sheet lying on top.

"Okay, so you need to sign here. Lanie will sign underneath and Stella will sign as your witness. Have either of you been married before?"

"Yes, both of us." Azarius reached into his inside pocket and pulled out the divorce decree.

"Great. I just need to make a copy of this for when I file," John said, grabbing it and turning to a small printer. "Hopefully, you have better luck with this one."

As the printer whirred to life and spat out a copy of his papers, Azarius signed his name to the line.

"Wonderful. If you'll come with me, I'll take you to the chapel room where we perform the ceremony and we can wait for Stella and Lanie."

Azarius followed John out of the office and down the hallway. He glanced back at the rooms, but Lanie's door was still closed. Was she backing out?

John took a right and Azarius followed him to a hallway enclosed by glass. It led to another large building he hadn't noticed from the front.

As John pushed open the door, the smell of flowers hit his nose. The room was set up similar to how he imagined a small church would look. Rows of white chairs lined both sides of a red carpeted aisle. A raised platform sat at the far back of the room surrounded by beautiful flowers in whites, pinks, and reds.

"Okay, here's where we'll stand," John said, stepping up on the platform. "Lanie will enter through that door, obviously, and when she gets here, we'll start the ceremony."

Azarius nodded and rolled his shoulders back. He wasn't nervous exactly, but he was ready to get the ceremony part over with. As the time crept on, he found himself rocking back and forth on his heels.

"I'm sure they're almost ready," John said with a kind smile.

Before Azarius could reply, the sound of music filled the room. The far door opened and Lanie stepped into view. She was a vision in her satin cream dress. The neckline dipped low and showed off her bare shoulders. Her auburn hair was piled loosely on her head with only a few tendrils hanging down. He was glad now that she hadn't modeled the dress for him in the store. He hadn't understood her adamant refusal then, but he did now. It would have ruined this moment.

She glided up the aisle, her dress skimming the floor. A bouquet of white roses clutched in her hands. A tentative smile adorned her face as she reached the podium and stepped up. When she turned to face him, Azarius realized they hadn't bought any rings. In a panic, he turned to John with wide eyes. John, seeming to understand his predicament, just smiled and held up a hand.

"Azarius and Lanie, you have come here today to declare your love for one another and pledge to spend your lives together. I haven't known either of you long, but I can see the love you have for each other, and I believe your union will be blessed and happy. Azarius, do you take Lanie to be your lawfully wedded wife, to have and to hold for as long as you both shall live?"

"I do," Azarius answered.

"Lanie, do you take Azarius as your husband to have and to hold as long as you both shall live?"

"I do," Lanie said, her eyes focused on Azarius.

John motioned Stella to join them on the podium. As she stepped up, Azarius realized she held a cushion with two thin gold bands on it. Of course, the package he had paid for had included rings. They were not what he wanted to symbolize their love forever, but they would work for now.

"Azarius, please take a ring and Lanie's hand and then repeat after me," John instructed.

Azarius grabbed the smaller gold band and Lanie's left hand.

"With this ring, I thee wed," John said and Azarius repeated the words, sliding the ring on Lanie's finger.

Lanie went next, sliding the ring on his finger as she repeated the words.

"By the power vested in me by the great state of Oklahoma, I now pronounce you husband and wife. You may kiss the bride."

Elated, Azarius leaned forward and placed his lips on Lanie's. They had kissed before, but it felt different this time with her as his wife, and from the look in her eyes as they pulled back, he knew she felt it too.

Stella tucked the pillow under her arm to clap. "Wonderful, so beautiful. Rosie has your cake ready, and I'd love to get a picture of the two of you for the wall."

Lacing his fingers through Lanie's, Azarius led the way down the aisle and back to the main building. Stella led them to a grand fireplace in the living room and they smiled for the camera before following her to the kitchen.

A small but pretty cake sat prominently displayed in the center of the large table.

"You want it here?" Stella asked. "Or I could send it up to your room with some dinner."

"Let's do that," Lanie said.

Azarius smiled and nodded his agreement. He was glad they were married, but hanging out with people he didn't know had never been his strong suit.

Stella led them back to their changing rooms where they grabbed their bags and then followed her up the stairs. She stopped in front of a white door at the end of the hall. "Here you go," she said, handing them a key on a large plastic frame. "I'll give you some time to get situated before I send up dinner and the cake."

"Thank you," Lanie said.

Stella smiled and nodded, then waved goodbye and headed back down the stairs.

"Well, shall we?" Azarius asked as he reached for the doorknob.

Lanie bit her lip and nodded. Azarius couldn't tell if she was excited, nervous, or both. The same emotions battled inside him as he opened the door.

A king-sized bed with a red comforter sat squarely in the middle of the room. White pillows floated at the top like clouds. On one pillow was a red rose and on another was a plate of chocolate covered strawberries. Azarius's stomach rumbled, and he realized he hadn't eaten in hours. Those strawberries would be at the top of his list.

Lanie stepped forward, but Azarius grabbed her arm before her foot could land in the room. She turned wide eyes on him as he smiled and scooped her into his arms.

"We might as well do this part right," he said and carried her over the threshold.

Lanie laughed as he set her down and then she reached behind her and closed the door.

Azarius picked up their bags, bringing them further into the room. A small couch sat under the window to the right and a table was on the left of the bed. Directly across from the bed was a wardrobe which probably housed a television along with some drawers.

Beyond the table was an open door, and Azarius stepped inside and flicked the light on. A large heart-shaped tub took up most of the real estate in the room, but there was also a toilet, a small sink, and a single person shower encased in glass.

Flicking off the light, he turned back around to face Lanie.

"Well, wife," he said, walking to her and putting his arms around her. "What would you like to do first?"

Her hands wound up around his neck and pulled him closer. "I think we should try out the strawberries and the bed," she said in a husky voice.

"A woman after my own heart," he said, dropping his lips to hers and backing her up until she fell onto the bed.

CHAPTER 13

*L*anie awoke in Azarius's arms and almost jumped out of bed before remembering they had gotten married the night before. With a small sigh, she rolled closer to him, enjoying the feel of his chest under her hand and his arm laying loosely around her.

One eye popped open, and he turned to her. "Hello wife, how did you sleep?"

"Surprisingly well," she said, running her hand over the faded tattoo on his chest. She had never noticed it before but the tattoo was of a pair of hands in a praying position. Perhaps Azarius was more religious than she originally thought.

"Surprisingly, huh?" A playful smile tugged at his lips as he pulled her closer and planted a kiss on her forehead. "That was the best sleep I've had in ages, but I'm not surprised. I knew you comforted and completed me."

Lanie smiled and snuggled down deeper against Azarius. "I suppose we should get up soon. I need to get back before my shift starts."

"Mmm, I don't want to get up yet. I won't get to make it down until Friday, and I'm not ready to let go of you yet."

"I don't want to get up yet either, but I'd also rather not anger my father any further."

That got Azarius moving. His eyes snapped open, and he pulled his arm away from Lanie, who immediately missed the warmth and security. "Come on," he said as he rolled over and planted his feet on the floor. "No way am I making your father hate me any more than he already does."

"He doesn't hate you," Lanie said as she stood beside him. "He dislikes the situation. You just happen to be a part of it, but maybe once he finds out we're married, the situation will resolve."

"Let's hope so, but until then, I'm not taking any chances."

❧

F our hours later, she was kissing him goodbye and climbing back in her car to return to Star Lake. It felt odd leaving this time. As much as she and Denny hadn't been a connected couple, they hadn't spent many nights in different places after they got married, and she felt as if she shouldn't be leaving Azarius. Perhaps she should move back to Dallas - she did have a job waiting for her, but she had just rented her house, and if she moved in with Azarius, there was still Greg to consider. She liked him as a person, but having him as a roommate while married didn't seem right.

Maybe one day Azarius would move to Star Lake, but she knew his job was important to him and the commute would be awful from her small town. Well, they'd figure it out. For now, weekends would have to work.

She pulled into her driveway later than she'd hoped. She had only thirty minutes to change and get to the store. With a quick flick of her wrist, she turned off the car and darted inside. There was no time for a full shower, but she peeled off her clothes and ran a wet rag across her face and under her arms.

Her reflection caught her attention in the mirror and she focused on her belly. It was pudgier than she remembered though not large. Lanie placed her hands on her tummy, but there was no movement. She wondered when she would begin to feel the fluttering sensations and then she remembered she hadn't set an appointment with the OB yet. Hopefully the store would be quiet enough she could sneak a call in to schedule it.

After pulling on a new pair of jeans and a clean shirt, Lanie raced back out of the house and to the ice cream shop. She unlocked the door with just minutes to spare.

Her first task was to take all the chairs down and give the tables another quick wipe. Then she needed to check the dishes and remove any from the dishwasher that had been washed before.

Lanie was in the middle of this process when the bell jingled and Bert walked in. "Hi, Bert, what can I do for you?"

Bert fumbled with his brown bow tie as he shuffled into the room. He wore a matching brown and cream checkered shirt and brown pants. "Hello, Lanie, I was wondering if you had a date to the Summer Fling next week."

"Aren't you seeing Amelia?" Lanie asked.

"Well, she said she needed a break, so I thought I'd see what else might be out there."

Lanie bit her lip to keep from smiling. It wasn't a romantic proposal even if she had been looking, so she was thrilled to have a real excuse to say no. "Oh, Bert, I appreciate the offer, but I'll have a date to the dance." At least she hoped she would. She had forgotten to ask Azarius, but as it was on a weekend, she assumed he would be there.

Bert's face crumpled in and Lanie felt bad for him. She didn't know Amelia well, but she hoped the girl would come around. The two seemed perfect for each other.

"I'm sorry Bert. Can I get you an ice cream? On the house?"

That appeared to lighten his load a little as he shuffled toward the bar and took a seat. "I'll have the triple chocolate brownie with caramel, fudge, and whip cream. Oh and don't forget the cherry."

Ah, their most expensive dessert on the menu. That made sense as to why it perked him up slightly. Lanie smiled and shook her head as she turned to scoop the dessert.

"Here you go, Bert," she said a few minutes later as she set the dessert in front of him.

"Thank you." He reached for the bowl, but

before he picked up the spoon, his eyebrows crammed together and he tilted his face up to hers. "Lanie, is that a wedding ring on your hand?"

"What?" Lanie glanced down at her left hand and froze as she realized she hadn't taken off the simple gold band from the night before. She thought about fibbing as quick remarriages were frowned upon nearly as much as unwed mothers in Star Lake, but she didn't want to start her marriage out with a lie. And people would know soon enough when she started to show. "It is, Bert. It's the reason I can't go with you to the dance. I married my friend Azarius last night."

Bert said nothing, but Lanie could see the wheels turning in his mind.

"That was quite fast," he finally managed and Lanie sighed. This would be a statement she had better get used to as she was bound to hear it more often in the future.

"Yes, I suppose it was, but sometimes you just know, right?"

He dipped his spoon in the dessert and brought it to his mouth. "Yes, I suppose you do," he mumbled through his bite.

Lanie sighed softly. Bert had been easy to

convince, but she knew there would be other people who would not be placated so easily.

When Bert finished his ice cream, he pushed the bowl back across the counter to her and left, leaving the parlor empty and Lanie able to call the nearest OB for an appointment. The nearest OB was almost an hour outside of town and was booked for the next two weeks, but Lanie didn't think that would be a problem. Nothing happened early in pregnancies, right?

As she hung up the phone, the bell above the door jingled and Paula made her entrance, her dark hair flying behind her.

"Lanie Perkins," she said, splaying her hands on the counter, "Bert just told me you got married yesterday. To whom did you marry and why were we not invited?"

Lanie sighed. She had hoped Bert would keep the information to himself or at the very least that he wouldn't run into Paula for a while, but secrets didn't remain secret very long in a small town. "I did, Paula. It was rather a spur-of-the-moment decision, but we will have a party soon and invite everyone."

"Do your parents know?" Paula asked, leaning back and cocking one hip to the side.

"Not yet, but I assume they will soon."

Paula's mouth dropped open at the implication of the snarky comment, and Lanie quickly hurried to amend the situation. The last thing she needed was Paula angry with her.

"Look, Paula, I'll tell my folks, but I'm thirty years old. I'm allowed to marry who I want when I want and I don't need anyone's permission."

That seemed to soothe Paula's fragile ego for the moment as her face softened and she leaned forward. "Was it at least that handsome friend of yours or did you pick up a random stranger on the street?"

Lanie let the dig go and smiled back at Paula. "It was my handsome friend whom I've actually known for years though we just recently began hanging out again after my separation. You can rest assured I didn't marry a stranger." As the words left her mouth, Lanie wondered how true they were. He had opened up about his ex-wife, but there was still so much in Azarius' past she didn't know, and she wondered how long it would take to peel away all the layers and finally feel like she knew him, the real him.

"Well, that is nice," Paula said, but her face told a different story. Lanie knew Paula would keep digging until she knew the real reason for the marriage.

After Paula, Lanie enjoyed a steady stream of customers. Some knew of her hasty marriage and asked questions, but others either didn't care or didn't know. Still, by the end of the evening, Lanie was exhausted.

A minute before closing time, the bell jingled again. Lanie nearly threw her hands up in frustration but smiled when she saw it was Layla. She gestured her inside and then locked the door behind her.

"I'm so glad it's just you. It's been busy tonight," Lanie said, sinking down into a chair and dropping her head onto her hands.

"For you or for Paula?" Layla joked as she pulled out the chair across from Lanie. Lanie groaned and rolled her eyes.

"You could have told me at least," Layla said. "I thought we were friends."

Lanie's head shot up. "Oh, Layla, I'm so sorry. I meant to tell you first, but I got in late today, and then Bert saw my ring and it just spiraled out of control from there."

"It's okay, I'm just teasing you. I guess that means the test was positive then?"

Lanie slapped her forehead. The stress of telling her parents and deciding what to do had weighed so heavily on her mind that she had forgotten to tell Layla. "Yes, but no one knows that part yet except for you and my parents. Azarius asked me to elope the night we told them. I wasn't going to at first, but then I thought about how people would react when I started to show, and I took him up on his offer."

Layla nodded, her dark hair rustling against her shoulders. "What about the secrecy thing? You guys work that out?"

Lanie's lips twisted together as she broke away from Layla's gaze. "Some, he told me about his ex-wife, but I didn't ask for more and he didn't volunteer any more. I'm hopeful now that we're married, he'll share his life with me."

A small sigh escaped Layla's lips. "I hope so for your sake, Lanie, but what are you going to do if he doesn't?"

Lanie shook her head. She had no idea.

CHAPTER 14

*A*zarius walked into his apartment with an extra bounce in his step. Some happy tune he couldn't place whistled from his lips.

"How did it go?" Greg asked from the couch.

"It was amazing. Lanie looked like an angel in her dress. I forgot rings, but they had simple bands for us," he said, looking down at the band on his left hand. Though small, the gold band stood out against his dark skin. "I'll have to get better ones soon as she deserves something with diamonds."

"Yes, she does. I'm glad you finally came around. Did you two have your heart to heart?"

Azarius shifted his weight and turned his face as he dropped his bag in the oversized chair. "Uh, not exactly. I told her about Krista but not my mama yet, but I will."

"You need to man. She deserves the truth, and she isn't going to run."

Azarius plopped down next to his bag. "I guess I know that, but I still worry, you know?"

"You don't have to worry about her. Lanie is all in when it comes to you as long as you stay all in."

As long as he stayed all in. That did seem to be his issue, didn't it? But this time would be different. He promised himself this time he was all in.

His day proved to be busy, but Lanie was never far from his mind. He waited as patiently as he could until nine pm when he knew she would be done at the diner before dialing her number. It rang two times before her angelic voice filled the earpiece.

"Hello?"

"Hello, wife, how was your day?" Azarius lay back against his black pillow and folded one arm behind his head.

There was a slight pause before she answered. "It was eventful. I forgot to take my ring off before I went to work and now half the town knows I got married."

"Well, that's okay, right? We knew they would find out eventually."

"Yeah, I guess I just wasn't expecting it to be so quickly." Another quick pause and her voice came again, lighter this time. "How was your day?"

A smile crawled across his lips. "It was great. I got to wake up with the most beautiful woman I know and call her my wife. The only thing that would have made it better was if I got to come home to her too."

"We'll have to figure that out soon. Oh hey, I scheduled the first appointment with the OB if you want to come. It's for the end of June. Also this weekend there's a Summer Fling. I know you say you don't dance in public, but would you be interested in going?"

Azarius's heart leapt. He wasn't much of a dancer, but the chance to see Lanie again and hold her in his arms was too good to pass up. "Of course I'm interested. You tell me when, and I'll be there. I'll stay the weekend if that works for you."

"I'd love that. I miss you already," she said.

"I miss you too." The feeling didn't go away as he hung up the phone. Instead, it intensified, growing and churning in his stomach. He couldn't remember ever feeling this way about a woman before, not even Krista.

When Friday finally rolled around, Azarius could barely wait for work to end so he could see Lanie again. Even though they had spoken every day of the week, it wasn't the same and he really wanted to hold her in his arms again. He missed the smell of her hair and the feel of her soft skin against his.

The house was dark as he pulled in, and he briefly wondered where Greg was, though it was possible he was sitting in the dark. He often did that when he had headaches, and he suffered from migraines often.

Azarius threw the Mustang in park and turned off the ignition. His plan was to be back on the road in half an hour, so he needed to pack a bag as quickly as possible. He should have done it last night, but work had run late, and he'd fallen into bed bone tired.

Not bothering to flick on the lights, he bounded up the stairs and clicked his bedroom light on. His bag still sat near the bed from the road trip to Oklahoma.

One at a time, he pulled open the drawers and grabbed the needed items. A few shirts, pants, socks, and underwear. Then he moseyed into the bathroom to grab his lotions, toothbrush, and shower items. He added those to the bag and grabbed a jacket for good measure. Mid-June in Texas normally meant warmer weather, but sometimes a cold front would sneak in, and he didn't want to be left unprepared.

As he opened the front door and stepped outside, he realized he still hadn't seen or heard Greg. Maybe he had gone to visit his folks. They did live close in town, so he could walk there if needed.

With a shrug of his shoulders, Azarius locked the door behind him and jogged back to the car. He had made great time and should see Lanie before she turned in for the night. The thought sent an extra tingle of joy through him and a smile across his lips. He turned the radio up and nodded his head to the beat as he pulled out of the driveway and back on the main road.

Two hours later, he was parking in front of Lanie's house. Her porch light gleamed, a welcoming beacon in the dark night. Reaching over, Azarius grabbed his bag and climbed out of the car, locking it behind him. The front door opened before he had a chance to knock and Lanie rushed into his arms.

The bag fell from his hand as he wound his arms around her and planted his lips on hers. Heat swirled through them, dispelling any chill in the surrounding air. When they broke apart, he smiled down at her. "I guess you did miss me."

"More than you know," she said. With her fingers firmly locked with his, she pulled him into the house, pausing only long enough for him to rescue his bag.

Sunlight streaming in through the windows woke Azarius the next morning. A glance to his left revealed Lanie's auburn hair splayed across his arm. He tightened his grip on her shoulder, relishing the feel of her against him. The realization that he had almost lost her made him squeeze her a little tighter, and she opened her eyes.

"Hey you," she said, her voice still heavy with sleep.

"Hey, sorry, I was enjoying the scent of your hair, go back to sleep."

She tilted her head to smile up at him. "What is it with you and my hair?"

"I don't know," he said, pushing her head back against his chest, "but yours has always smelled fantastic."

A giggle escaped her lips, and she batted his chest playfully. "I love you, funny man."

The words permeated his heart and a feeling of joy coursed through his body.

"We should probably get up," Lanie said as her finger lazily traced a pattern on his chest. "My parents probably know, but we should stop in and tell them before the dance in case they don't."

That sounded like torture to Azarius, but he would do anything for Lanie, and so after another kiss on her forehead, he released her from his grip. She leaned up and planted her lips directly on his, nibbling slightly on his bottom lip and sending a tingling sensation through him.

"You better stop that if you want to get up," he said.

She winked at him, but pulled back, and he immediately missed the warmth. Sighing, he rolled over and out of the bed.

As Lanie padded to the shower, he wandered into the kitchen to make some tea. He filled the tea kettle and set it boiling on the stove while he opened cupboards in search of some tea bags. Lanie loved green tea almost as much as her coffee, so she was sure to have a few bags around somewhere. His search yielded a stash in the pantry, and he pulled out the box.

Lanie entered the kitchen as the tea kettle began

whistling. "Shower's free," she said, planting a kiss on his cheek.

"I'll jump in as soon as I finish my tea," he said, returning her kiss and filling a mug.

She filled a mug as well and sat down at the small table across from him. As he sipped the warm tea and took in her porcelain skin from across the way, he knew he could no longer be content with only seeing her on weekends. He'd have to make the decision to either move here with her or convince her to move back with him, but it could wait until after the dance tonight. Maybe by then he'd have an idea of what to do.

A few hours later, they pulled up in front of Lanie's parents' house. Though they were married now, Azarius's mouth still dried up at the prospect of seeing her father again.

"Come on, it can't be any worse than last time," Lanie said, sensing his discomfort.

"Yeah, I know," he said with a shrug. "I just wish we could win them over."

"We will one day," she said and turned off the engine.

The walk up to the door felt like the green mile to Azarius. Lanie squeezed his hand as she rang the doorbell. Again her mother was the one to answer it.

"Lanie, Azarius, come on in," her mother said with a smile, but Azarius noted it didn't quite reach her eyes.

"Hi mom, sorry we didn't call first, and you've probably already heard the news, but Azarius and I wanted to make sure you heard it from us before you were accosted at the dance."

"I'm not sure to what news you are referring," her mother said. "But you should share with your father too."

They followed the older woman into the living room. Lanie's father looked up as they entered. "Well, hello again. To what do we owe this pleasure?"

Lanie opened her mouth to speak, but Azarius stepped forward and spoke first. "We wanted to say again how sorry we are that we didn't do things right the first time, but I took your words to heart. The Army taught me to follow through with commitments and so Lanie and I eloped last weekend. We hope you'll be able to give us your blessing now as we want to move forward."

Her mother clasped her hand to her mouth and collapsed into a chair. "Oh, Lanie, you eloped?"

"It was my idea, ma'am. I wanted Lanie to be

married before she started showing and people began asking questions."

"But we plan to have a big party to announce it mom," Lanie said, stepping in.

There was a moment of silence as her parents looked back and forth at each other. Then her father rose from his chair and approached. "Army, huh? What's your rank, son?"

"I'm a sergeant, and I'm still in the reserves sir."

Bob's eyes narrowed even more. "Well, I certainly can appreciate your service. I too served my country. One more question. What is your stance on God?"

"Dad," Lanie said with a shake of her head.

Azarius took a deep breath. "To be honest sir, until I met Lanie, I believed there was a God, but I didn't have a relationship with him. However, after hearing your daughter talk about him and seeing her faith, I started looking and praying." He smiled as Lanie turned to him with wide eyes. "I hadn't told you yet, but I did. I started praying, and with your help, I'd like to deepen that relationship. I know I may not know exactly how to be a strong leader yet, but I'd like to try."

Lanie's father narrowed his eyes as if he were trying to decide if Azarius were telling the truth. Lanie's bottom lip was curled in under her top teeth as she looked from her father to Azarius and back again.

"I don't approve of the way this started, but I do see that you are trying to make a difference," her father said. He extended his hand. "Welcome to the family."

Relief flooded Azarius as he shook the outstretched hand. Maybe they could be a real family after all.

CHAPTER 15

*L*anie couldn't believe how well the interaction with her parents had gone. "Were you serious about what you said about praying?" she asked Azarius as she backed out of her parents' drive.

"I was and I am," he said with a smile that showed off his white teeth. "Are you pleased?"

"Pleased and surprised," she said as she pulled into a space in front of The Diner. "I honestly thought that might be the one thing we'd fight over in the future."

"Well, now we have nothing to fight over," he said, flashing a wink at her.

"Good, now come and meet my friends. I want to show you off." She parked the car and opened the door, but as she stepped out a pain shot through her abdomen and she doubled over.

Azarius rushed to her side, concern etched on his face. "Are you alright?"

She took a deep breath, hoping to ease the pain. "Yeah, I think I'm just hungry." The pain receded, and she stood, flashing him what she hoped was a confident smile, but he didn't look convinced. "Come on, it's nothing."

Lanie led the way into The Diner, waving to the people she knew as she made her way over to the back booth Layla was holding down. She slid in across from Layla and patted the seat next to her for Azarius to sit.

"Layla, I want you to officially meet my husband, Azarius. Azarius, this is my friend Layla."

"It's nice to meet the man who's made my friend smile again," Layla said as she shook Azarius's hand.

He nodded, forcing a smile on his face, but Lanie could still see the concern residing in his eyes.

Max appeared a few minutes later, clad in his usual flannel. "Back for food this time, huh?" he asked Azarius as he plopped three menus on the table top.

"Max, behave," Layla said, raising her eyebrow at him. "This is Azarius, Lanie's husband."

Something akin to a snort came out of Max's mouth as he leaned back and folded his arms across his chest. "Husband, huh? Well, congrats I guess."

"Thanks, Max," Lanie said. "Maybe our nuptial will spur you into action, huh?" She cringed again as Layla kicked her shin under the table, but it was worth it. If her friend wasn't going to push him, someone ought to.

Max opened his mouth to speak, but thought better of it and turned back to the kitchen without a word.

"Is that guy the owner?" Azarius asked in a hushed voice.

Layla belted out a laugh, throwing back her head and letting her dark hair swish back and forth. "Yeah, he's the owner. He's a little gritty on the outside, but he's really a sweetheart underneath all that gruff."

"Max is Layla's boyfriend," Lanie explained.

"Oh, I see." Azarius unfolded the menu and glanced over the contents.

"Yeah, he is an acquired taste," Layla said with a smile.

Lanie grinned back before another shock of pain shot through her. She tried to keep her face passive as she reached over and pushed on her abdomen. It was odd to have cramps if she were pregnant, wasn't it?

As the pain receded again, she pushed the thought from her mind and decided to enjoy lunch with her friends. After this it would be time to get ready for the Summer Fling Dance and she had the perfect dress. She couldn't wait to show Azarius.

Two hours later, Lanie was curled up on the couch watching cartoons with Azarius. She wasn't much for cartoons herself, but if it meant laying in his arms, she didn't care what they watched. As she looked up at him though, an old doubt resurfaced and tumbled from her mouth before she could stop it.

"Azarius, why didn't you tell me your birthday the first time I asked?"

"Huh?"

He kept his face turned to the television, but she had felt him stiffen slightly and she knew he had heard her. Well, two could play this game. She maneuvered to a sitting position, so she was blocking his vision.

"You heard me. Why didn't you tell me when your birthday was?"

He sighed and shifted his glance to her eyes. "I told you, I don't want anyone to make a big deal of my birthday because I don't reciprocate well. I'll probably forget yours at least once in this marriage."

"I know, but that doesn't seem like the real reason or at least not the whole reason. I just want the truth."

"That is the truth, Lanie," he said.

She knew there was more and the fact he wouldn't tell her miffed her. "Fine, I thought you were going to open up to me, share your life, but I guess not." She stood and walked to the bedroom, her feet stomping on the floor harder than she intended.

"Lanie." She heard his voice behind her, but she shut the door and locked it, blocking out his noise. As she did, another wave of pain coursed through her abdomen and she fell against the bed, clutching her stomach. She might be angry at him for concealing the whole truth, but wasn't she doing the same thing?

The pain had gotten worse, but she hadn't told him about it and she didn't even know why. Shouldn't she be sharing everything with him now that he was her husband? Yet, she couldn't stop from telling herself that she'd take care of it Monday after he left, that surely it wasn't anything to worry about. She fell asleep with that thought in her head, curled up with her hands over her stomach.

Incessant knocking at her door woke Lanie sometime later. She opened her eyes, concentrating on her stomach, but the pain was gone. At least for now. Rolling off the bed, she trundled to the door and opened it.

"I don't want to fight, Lanie, I'm sorry," Azarius said. "I'll tell you whatever you want to know."

Lanie shook her head as she stepped into his arms. "No, I should be the one apologizing. I know you'll tell me when you're ready." *Just like I'll tell you about the pain when I'm ready.*

His arms wound around her, and Lanie sighed against his muscular chest. "It's almost time for the dance. You still want to go?" She tilted her head up to look at him.

He leaned down to place a kiss on her nose. "I'll go wherever you want to go. I know I'm not the best at expressing my feelings, but I promise to work on it."

"It means everything, right?" she said with a smile, remembering the song he had once sent her via text.

His arms tightened around her. "That's right. It

means everything."

An hour later, Lanie and Azarius walked arm and arm into the large red barn. Pink, white, and blue balloons hung from the ceiling amid streamers of the same color. A few tables filled the right side, each covered in a different table cloth cover. Amid those, a small table with a speaker system blared songs for those on the dance floor. At the very back, a long table was laden with a myriad of cookies and bowls of fruit punch.

"Never see anything like this back in Dallas, huh?" Lanie said, squeezing Azarius's arm.

"There might be a reason for that," Azarius said with a smile.

Lanie punched his arm and led him to the dance floor.

"Lanie, I don't dance in public," Azarius said, planting his feet.

"You do today. Come on, it's a slow song. You just put your arms around me and sway. Please." She put on her best puppy dog face and batted her eyes at him.

He rolled his eyes and shook his head, but followed her to the floor. "Fine, but don't say I didn't warn you."

As his arms wound around her, Lanie breathed in his manly scent, put her head on his shoulder, and sighed. The grey shirt he was wearing tonight hugged his chest and his arms, accentuating his well-toned muscles. She couldn't imagine any place she'd rather be.

"See, this isn't too ha….." Lanie never finished her sentence as the worst pain yet shot through her stomach. Her hand clutched at Azarius's arm as she crumpled downward.

"Lanie? What's wrong?"

Lanie shook her head, the pain too strong to talk over. With a strength she didn't know he had, Azarius scooped her up in his arms and headed for the door.

"What's going on?" Layla's concerned voice reached Lanie's ears as the cooler air hit her skin.

"I don't know," Azarius said. "She just collapsed, holding her stomach. She's grabbed it a few times today. Where's the closest doctor?"

"Closed for now, but there's an ER clinic on the far side of town. Come on, I'll drive."

"Where are we going?" Max's voice had joined the conversation.

"The ER, come on."

Moments later the car door opened and Lanie felt Azarius sliding her into the backseat. Then he climbed in beside her. The feel of his hands smoothing her hair warmed her heart. She remembered a time a few months back when she had done the same for him.

He hadn't wanted her to come over, insisting he didn't feel well, but Lanie had promised to work and let him rest. When she got there, he had curled up on the couch with his head on her lap and she had stroked it until he felt better. It had been a loving gesture then, but she had never expected the gesture to be returned.

The car roared to life, and Lanie could tell by the erratic driving that Layla was behind the wheel. A few minutes later, Lanie rolled forward as Layla slammed on the brake and threw the car into park.

Azarius helped her out of the car before picking her up again and striding into the ER.

"Can I help you?" a woman's voice said.

"My wife is having stomach pains, and she's pregnant."

"She's what?" Max's voice broke through the haze of pain.

"Sssh! Not now."

Layla's voice hushing Max was the last thing Lanie heard before the darkness took her over.

CHAPTER 16

When Lanie opened her eyes, the first thing she noticed was the cold, numb sensation inside her veins. The awful searing pain was gone, but the emptiness in its place was even worse. It reminded her of that old Robert Frost poem "Fire and Ice." She had always thought the fire would be the worse, but she would gladly trade the ice she felt now for the earlier fire. She splayed her hands across her abdomen, but there was nothing.

It's just too early, that's all. I didn't feel anything yesterday either.

But the truth nibbled at her brain. The pain earlier hadn't been natural. Even though this was her first pregnancy, she knew that. Of course she knew that, but God wouldn't take her baby, would he?

Not when she had come back to the fold. What was that old story? The one about the shepherd who rejoices when the lost sheep returns or the prodigal son. That's what she was - the prodigal daughter. And Azarius had started praying. Surely that gave them some points, some cushion from the grief of life. He might never have started praying had there been no baby.

"Lord, I know we didn't do it right in the beginning, but if you'll save this baby, I promise we'll do it right from now on. We'll be there every Sunday. We'll attend Bible studies. I'll join the choir. We'll do whatever you want us to do if you'll save the baby."

Lanie waited for some warmth, some sign of healing, but the cold emptiness remained. Maybe God was no longer listening. Maybe he had turned his back on her because of her divorce and her sexual slipup.

"Ah, you're awake."

Lanie turned to the door. An elderly nurse with a kind face and blue scrubs smiled at her.

"How are you feeling?"

"Cold," Lanie replied.

"Oh, well, let me get you a blanket."

Lanie nodded, though she knew no blanket would warm up the cold she felt.

The nurse exited the room and returned a moment later with a folded blanket in her arms. "Here you go, fresh out of the warmer. That should help."

She spread the blanket over Lanie's body, but it made no difference. The bitter cold still ate at her insides.

"You have people waiting to see you, but I'll send the doctor in first, okay?"

"Is it gone?" Though Lanie was certain she had lost the pregnancy, she needed to hear the words.

The woman's face held her smile, but her eyes dropped a little. "I'll send in the doctor to talk to you shortly."

She exited the room, leaving Lanie in silence. She hadn't said yes, Lanie reasoned. Maybe the baby wasn't gone; maybe there were just complications. She could handle complications, but the loss? If the baby was gone, would Azarius be gone too? As much as she wanted to believe he had married her for her, a shred of doubt that the marriage had occurred only because of the baby remained.

The door opened, and a young man in a white coat entered. He didn't look much older than Lanie, except for his receding hairline. "Hello, Lanie, I'm Dr. Fredrickson, how are you feeling?"

A darkness like nothing she'd felt before descended on Lanie, and her eyes narrowed. "Why does everyone keep asking me that? How do you think I'm feeling?"

The doctor appeared not to register her anger as his voice did not change in emotion or inflection. "I'm sure you are feeling a lot of things. Probably guilt and anger at the loss of your pregnancy."

Lanie squeezed her eyes shut and shook her head. *No, it wasn't true.* If she didn't listen to him, it wouldn't be true.

"And those feelings are completely normal," he continued. "But Lanie, it's important that you also know this wasn't your fault. It was an ectopic pregnancy. It never had a chance, and the pain you felt today was your body rejecting it. The good news is that it didn't rupture, and there appears to be no damage to your fallopian tubes so you'll be able to get pregnant again. In fact, a lot of women get pregnant within months of a miscarriage like this."

Lanie continued to shake her head. Waves of denial and anger fought within her.

"I'll give you some time, but your family would like to see you."

Family. The word elicited a single tear from her right eye. She had no family. Her chance at a family had died with the fire and only the ice remained, and the ice was so much worse.

Azarius paced the floor of the hospital, worry lines etched in his face. He needed word on Lanie's condition. In his brain, he knew it wasn't cancer, but he couldn't help fearing he'd lose Lanie just like he'd lost his mother. He didn't think he would survive if something happened to her.

A young doctor approached the waiting area. "Azarius Jacobson?" he asked after glancing at his clipboard.

"That's me," Azarius said and Lanie's two friends joined him.

"Well, physically your wife is going to be fine. She's resting now. Emotionally though, well, you need to speak with her. Lanie's not herself right now, and she might not be for a while. She's going to need time and a lot of patience."

"Can I see her?"

"Yes, but I suggest one at a time, and remember patience." He motioned for Azarius to follow him down the sterile hallway.

This, this was the green mile. Azarius had thought the walk to her parents' house had been bad, but the fear and sadness he felt now were so much worse.

Azarius knocked gently on the door before pushing it open. Lanie lay still and stiff under the white sheet. She glanced his way as he entered and then returned her focus to the television up on the wall which was playing some game show. He wondered what she was thinking behind her expressionless face.

"Hey Lanie. How are you?" he asked when he reached her bedside.

"I lost our baby, Azarius, how do you think I'm feeling?"

"We… we lost the baby?" He couldn't keep the shock from his voice. The baby was gone. The baby that had brought them together. Did that mean they would fall apart now? Or were they strong enough to survive this? Fear they weren't flooded his veins.

"Not we, Azarius. Me. I lost the baby. It was ectopic."

Azarius blinked at the flat tone of her voice. He had never heard her normally bright cheery voice so empty.

"It wasn't your fault, Lanie," he said reaching for her hand. Though she didn't pull it away, she made no move to return the gesture and her hand remained limp like wilted lettuce in his hand. "It it was an ectopic pregnancy, there was nothing you could have done."

"It's our punishment, don't you see? We're being punished for intimacy outside of marriage."

Azarius sighed and sat down on the edge of the bed. "Lanie, I know I'm new to this religion thing, but I don't think God works that way. Ectopic pregnancies happen all the time. Did the doctor say anything else?"

"He said there was no damage, that we'd be able to try again."

"Well, that's a good thing. I'd say we're lucky then."

"Lucky?" she snorted. "We eloped to save ourselves from the embarrassment of having a child out of wedlock, and now there is no child."

Azarius shook his head. His words were coming out all wrong. "Lanie, I don't care about all of that," he began.

"You don't care about our baby?" Lanie's voice dripped with venom as she turned fiery eyes on him. "That's all we had holding us together."

"That's not true."

"It is true, and you know it!" Her voice rose in

volume until the last two words were almost shouted. "You know what? Just get out."

"Lanie…"

"Out!" she screamed. "You can go back to your secrecy and riddles and the other women you probably have on the side."

Azarius sucked in his breath. She's not herself, he had to remind himself. "I'll go for now, Lanie, but I'm not leaving forever."

She said nothing, just returned her gaze to the television.

Unsure what else to do, Azarius sighed and exited the room.

Layla stood as he entered the waiting room. "How did it go?"

Azarius shook his head. Tears stung the back of his throat, but he would not cry in front of this woman he barely knew.

"It's okay," she said, touching his arm. "She's hurting right now, but it will get better."

Azarius nodded and covered her hand with his own to show he understood. Then he walked down the hall. He needed to be alone.

He rounded the corner and leaned against the wall, but before he could let the emotions out, his phone rang. The area code was Dallas, but he didn't recognize the number. Swallowing the knot of emotion in his throat, he punched the button.

"Hello?"

"Is this Azarius Jacobson?"

The unfamiliar professional voice dispelled the last of his emotion, and he stood straighter. "Yes, this is Azarius."

"Mr. Jacobson, we have you listed as an emergency contact for Greg Weaver."

Azarius's heart tightened. "Yes, is everything okay?" This couldn't be happening. First Lanie and now Greg.

"He was in an accident last night."

"I'm on my way," Azarius said, not waiting for more details from the woman. He looked around and spying a nurse at a nearby desk, he headed her direction.

"Hi, do you have some paper, so I can leave a note?"

The woman held up a finger and only then did he see the phone attached to her ear. Nodding, he stepped away from the desk to give her some privacy to finish the call.

"I'm sorry, what did you need?" she asked a moment later.

"Some paper to leave a note."

She looked down at the desk which was cluttered with papers and shifted through them until she found a blank one. She handed it to him with a pen and then turned to her computer.

Azarius scribbled a quick message to Lanie about Greg's accident and folded the paper. "Can you make sure the patient in room 108 gets this?"

The nurse nodded, but as she took the paper, Azarius wondered if his folded slip wouldn't get lost in the clutter of the desk. With a sigh, he headed for the exit, dialing a cab on his way. Lanie needed him, but she didn't want him around right now, and he needed to make sure Greg was okay. Maybe the drive would clear his head and he would find some way to convince Lanie he wasn't going anywhere.

CHAPTER 17

*A*zarius entered Greg's room in the Dallas hospital both anxious to make sure Greg was okay and take him to task for his poor timing.

Greg's right leg was suspended in the air, encased in a cast and a bandage was wrapped around his head as well.

"Dude, what happened?" All thoughts of giving Greg a hard time flew from his mind at the image of his friend broken and battered.

Greg's lips pulled into a lopsided smile. "It's worse than it looks, really. Az, I met a girl."

"Where? In the hospital?" Azarius wondered if the head trauma was affecting Greg's memory.

"No, last night. I met her after work. I called an

Uber for a ride home, and she was the driver. She's beautiful, Az. Long dark hair and emerald eyes."

"That's great, Greg, but what about the accident?"

"Oh, yeah, we got in a heated discussion about the best television show, and she missed a stop sign. Neither of us saw the other truck."

"I hope she has insurance," Azarius said.

"I'm sure she does, but it's not like that, man. She's been here every moment since the accident."

Azarius glanced around the room to make sure he hadn't missed the beautiful mystery woman. "Greg? How much head trauma did you sustain? There's no one here."

"She went to get some food. She'll be right back."

As if his words held summoning power, a woman entered the doorway. "Oh, sorry, I didn't know you had guests. I can come back later."

"No, Jada, this is my bro, Azarius, the one I told you about."

Jada's eyes lit up, and a smile stretched across her face. She hurried into the room, dropping the food on the table before coming to Azarius's side. Before he knew what was happening, she had grabbed his hand and was pumping it up and down.

"I'm so happy to meet you. Greg has told me such

good things, and I know you must be worried about me, but I'm normally a very good driver, and I do have insurance so Greg will be taken care of." The words spilled out one after the other from her mouth and all Azarius could do was stare. He had never heard anyone speak so quickly.

"I wish we had met under different circumstances, but Greg said you were visiting your wife." Her hand flew to her mouth. "Oh, I'm so sorry we cut your visit short. Yours was the only name I had before we got in the accident. I guess his license still shows his sister's place, and they tried to call her, but she wasn't answering, so then they asked me if he had any other family as he had a brain bleed and they thought they might have to do surgery. He had called you his brother; I didn't realize you aren't brothers by blood, but I told them to look you up. I didn't mean to ruin your weekend though."

The irony of this woman, who appeared to have only one speed when she spoke, liking Greg, who rarely spoke full sentences, hit Azarius and he laughed. A full bellied, throaty laugh that pushed away his sadness and fears for a moment.

Jada's eyes grew wide, and she glanced to Greg, who appeared just as surprised as she was.

"I'm sorry," Azarius said, composing himself. "It's

just that you two are like polar opposites, which probably means you're perfect for each other. It's nice to meet you, Jada, and you're right - I do wish we had met under better circumstance, but if Greg likes you, then I like you." He turned to Greg. "And what about you? What is the damage here?"

"Broken leg, concussion, mild brain bleed, and bruised ribs," Greg said. "I'll live."

"You will, but you'll need someone to take care of you and I can't stay. Lanie had an ectopic pregnancy and lost it."

Jada sucked in her breath. "Oh no."

"Oh man, I'm sorry," Greg said. "Is she doing okay?"

"Not really," Azarius said with a shake of his head. "She's angry and hurt. I need to show her I'm not going anywhere."

"How are you going to do that?" Greg asked.

"By doing something I should have done a long time ago. I'm going to tell her the truth. And I'm going to commit. I'm going all in, but it means I won't be in the apartment to take care of you."

"I can do it," Jada said. "I don't believe in living together, but I can check up on him, and I'll pay for someone to be there with him when I can't."

Azarius turned to her. "How can you afford that on an Uber driver pay?"

"It pays more than you think," she laughed, "but it wouldn't be paid with my Uber pay." She bit her lip as if unsure if she wanted to disclose the thought on her mind, then drew her shoulders back and looked him in the eye. "I'm an heiress. My father owns Vizio Technology. I don't drive because I have to; I drive because I want to. It keeps me grounded, and I like meeting all the different types of people."

Now Azarius knew they were a match made in Heaven. For all of Greg's positives, handling money was not one of them. Azarius looked to Greg.

"It will be fine, man. I know it seems fast, but when you know, you know, right?"

Azarius nodded. He felt the same way about Lanie. It might have taken them a decade to get together, but he'd known she was special the first time he saw her. "Okay, well, can I get you anything from the house? I'm going to start getting things in order and then take care of some business tomorrow."

The shop he needed to visit would be closed tonight, but hopefully they'd be open tomorrow. He didn't want to be away from Lanie for long, especially in her present state. She might think she didn't want or need him, but he was determined to show her differently.

"Yeah, I could use a few things," Greg said, "but just drop them by tomorrow. I can't use any of them tonight anyway."

Azarius took notes on his phone of the items Greg would need for the next few days and then headed to the apartment.

As he stepped inside, he realized it might be one of his last times in the place. He wouldn't miss the apartment per se- it was nothing fancy - but it did hold memories of his time with Lanie, and while he knew he would be making more memories, a sentimental piece tugged at his heart.

He gathered up Greg's items and then packed a bag of his own. He would probably have to hire someone to pack up the rest of the items, but that could wait. Three months still remained on the lease.

After those tasks were finished, Azarius climbed into bed. Only the faintest whiff of Lanie's shampoo remained on his pillow, and he missed her warmth.

"Lord," he said quietly, "please be with Lanie now. Comfort her and heal her pain. Work on her heart and help me to know exactly what to say to show her how serious I am."

✿

"He's not here?" Lanie asked as Layla helped her pack up the next morning. There wasn't much, but Layla had run to her house the previous night and grabbed toiletries and comfortable clothing. She had then stayed until visiting hours ended when Lanie had been left alone with her thoughts.

Torturous, sad, and lonely thoughts. Yet, somewhere in the midst of those thoughts, an arm of comfort had surrounded her, easing the guilt and numbing the pain. Just as He stated in the Bible, God had been there at her lowest, offering her comfort if only she would accept it

It wasn't an immediate erasing of pain, and Lanie knew there would still be rough days ahead, but she had woken this morning with a desire to apologize to Azarius. He certainly hadn't earned the lashing she delivered the night before.

Layla bit her bottom lip and shook her head. "No, I'm sorry, honey. I haven't seen him since last night. He seemed pretty shaken up though."

Lanie's lips pursed together forming a tight seal. Of course he was. She had told him to leave and practically kicked him out of the room and out of her life. "Well, that's a problem for another day, I guess," Lanie said. She had no more energy to give today.

Layla placed her arm on Lanie's shoulders. "I don't think he's gone for good. One thing I can tell for sure is when a man loves a woman, and he loves you."

"Right," Lanie nodded, "that's why it took a decade for you to realize Max loved you."

Layla feigned shock before throwing her head back and laughing. "Well, maybe I can't see it when it's aimed at me, but I can tell with anyone else." Her laughter rang throughout the room - a ray of hope in the midst of the darkness, and Lanie tucked that ray of hope away to remember later when the sadness knocked again.

"All ready?" An elder orderly with closely cropped grey hair pushed a black wheelchair into the room.

"Is that really necessary?" Lanie asked with a roll of her eyes. "I can walk."

A single shake of his head confirmed her fears. "Sorry, hospital policy. Everyone gets a ride out. Think of it as curbside service."

He flashed a wink and a smile, earning a small one in return. With a sigh, Lanie walked to the chair and sat down.

"Now that wasn't so hard, see?" He patted her

shoulder with a tan, weathered hand that had probably comforted many patients before her. Then he turned the chair around and pushed it out the door.

It felt good to leave the sterile walls, but hard. This building held the last memory of her child, but also the realization she'd never know if she had lost a son or a daughter.

Before the black cloud could cloak her again, Lanie pushed the thought away and squared her shoulders. It would do no good to dwell in the past. She needed to focus on the future, whatever it might hold.

Lanie stood in front of her bathroom mirror Monday wondering if she really could go into work. Her father had offered to give her a few days, but she'd insisted the business of routine would help her feel better. Now she wasn't so sure.

Dark circles still clung to her eyes, and a sadness she wasn't used to seeing had taken residence on her face. Part of it was losing the baby, but another part was not hearing from Azarius. She knew she had been hard on him, but she had hoped he would fight for their marriage, that he would be there to take her home or at least call to check up on her, but none of that had happened.

His arms could have at least eased some of the pain on her heart. After all, it was his baby too. She looked back to the warm comfort of her bed which beckoned to her with soft sheets and the promise of cloaking darkness. She could crawl in bed, pull the covers over her head, and let the darkness steal the rest of the day. Her father would understand.

The chime of the doorbell halted her decision. She wasn't expecting anyone, but it was probably her mother checking up on her. Not bothering to even brush her hair, Lanie shuffled to the front door and pulled it open.

Still raw with emotion, tears streamed down her face before words could form at the vision in front of her. Azarius stood with his arms by his side and a bag at his feet, an angel in the midst of the wilderness.

"I thought you were gone," Lanie sobbed. Her knees gave out, but before she could hit the floor, he stepped over the threshold and wound his arms around her.

"For better or for worse, remember?" he whispered in her ear and Lanie melted into his strong chest, letting his arms bear most of her weight. The tears poured out, a continuing landslide of tears down her cheeks and still he held her. He held her until her shoulders stopped shaking and her breath slowed. Only then did he lift her face to look in her eyes.

"Where did you go?" she asked. "Why weren't you there when I was released?"

Azarius kissed her nose. "Let me bring my bag in and I'll tell you everything."

Reluctantly, Lanie stepped from his embrace and let him grab his bag and shut the door. Azarius patted his pocket and grabbed Lanie's hand, leading her to the couch.

"I left you a note, but I'm guessing from your reaction you never got it."

Lanie shook her head.

Azarius nodded; he should have known as much. "After you told me go," he began, "I got a call from a Dallas hospital. Greg had been in an accident and they couldn't reach his sister."

"Oh no, is he okay?" Lanie asked, squeezing Azarius's hand tighter.

"He will be," Azarius said. "He'll have some healing to do, but he met a new friend who I think will take good care of him. Lanie, I know you wanted me to leave, but I hope it was only the anger talking."

Lanie nodded; she still couldn't believe how she had lashed out at him. "It was mostly that, but," her eyes dropped to her lap.

"But what?" His finger tilted her chin up again. "You can tell me anything."

"I was… I am afraid that now that there's no baby, you won't want to be married any longer. There's still so much you haven't told me, and I…" her words trailed off.

Azarius sighed. "Lanie, I know the baby is what brought us together, but it wasn't the reason I married you. That night, that fateful bad decision night, I knew I was falling for you. It broke my heart when I saw your note the next morning, and when you first left for Star Lake, I was a mess. I had no idea how much I cared about you until you were gone."

He shook his head and smiled. "You can ask Greg - well, when he gets out of the hospital. I moped around all day and spent most of the time in my room in the dark. It was Greg who convinced me to drive out to see you that first time, and I didn't even know about the baby then, but I knew I wanted to be with you. But you didn't seem ready, and I thought I'd lost you again. Then you showed up on my doorstep with the news of your pregnancy, and I was terrified and elated at the same time. I knew this was our chance, but I tried to play it safe, to keep my secrets and live in both sides, and I've realized I can't do that."

Lanie bit the inside of her lip. She wanted to ask him to spill it, just get to the meat, but she forced herself to listen. He was finally opening up to her the way she had wanted from the first day, and she wasn't going to mess that up.

Azarius took a deep breath and blew it out. His eyes dropped to their hands, and he laced their fingers together before meeting her eyes again. "I told you once that I lost my mother when I was very young. It was actually the morning after my tenth birthday. She was sick with cancer, but I didn't know that. She had hidden it from me because we were poor and she couldn't afford the expensive treatments."

Pieces began to click into place. Of course he would have a negative association with his birthday, who wouldn't?

"I woke up that morning to a quiet house which was unusual. Even on her worst days, my mama would be up and fixing breakfast when I woke up, but that morning it was quiet. I knew something was wrong, and I went to her room. She lay in bed, looking peaceful, and I thought she was just asleep but after shaking her and hollering for her to wake up, I knew something was wrong, but I had no one to call, so I climbed up in bed with her and lay there until the neighbor showed up."

Lanie sucked in her breath and tears welled up in her eyes. "I'm so sorry, Azarius. Is that why you avoid your birthday?"

"I don't avoid it," he said.

"Yes, you do," she countered.

"Okay, I guess I do. Those memories are hard to deal with every year, so I found if I treated it like any other day, it got easier. Anyway, the neighbor came and took me to her house for the afternoon, but then CPS came. I had no idea who my father was, and most of my mother's family were either dead or too poor to take me in, so I landed in foster care. Some places were better than others, but on the whole it wasn't an experience I would want to repeat. It taught me to hold information close and keep people at a distance.

"Then I landed at Mary's house - my mother. She had just married, but found out she couldn't have kids and so she decided to foster in hopes of adopting. I was thirteen and a handful, but she kept me anyway, even after the divorce of her first husband. My mom and I became close friends, and little by little she got me to open up."

"I don't understand then," Lanie said, interrupting him. "If your mom got you to open up, why are you still so distant?"

"I wasn't finished," Azarius said with a smile. "I didn't have many close relationships, but it's because I was looking for someone like my mother. When I met you, I thought I had finally found someone I could open up to. Before I could tell you though, you were engaged and then married, and my world was thrown upside down again."

"Azarius, I never knew," Lanie interrupted. Would it have made a difference, she wondered?

"I know you didn't, and that was my fault. I should have told you in the beginning, but I was too scared to. Krista was the first person I opened up to, and you know what happened with her. Needless to say, my trust in people diminished about then. The only person I've told since is Greg, and that's only because I met him right after Krista left me and he helped me through some hard times. I'm sorry I didn't tell you earlier, but I need you to know that I love you and when you collapsed, I was reminded of my mother again. All I could think was that I needed you to be okay because I couldn't... I can't imagine my life without you."

Tears began to stream out of the corner of Lanie's eyes.

"Hey, hey, why are you crying? I thought me being open was what you wanted."

"It is," she sniffled. "Now I can really see a future with you, but the baby..."

He wiped a tear from her cheek. "I know. I'm sad about the baby too, but we have plenty of time to start a family. In fact, we have the rest of our lives to do that, if you'll let me stick around." He reached into his pocket and pulled out a small black box. "I'm glad we got married when we did, but I always regretted not having a better ring for you."

Lanie gasped as he opened the lid. A beautiful sparkly diamond sat nestled in between intertwining rings of silver and gold. "Oh, Azarius," she said with a sigh. "It's perfect. It means everything."

He smiled as he slipped her old band off and slid the new ring on her finger. "You mean everything."

With no words left to say, Lanie circled her arms around his neck and met his lips.

"Ugh, nothing fits," Lanie said, throwing yet another skirt on the bed. Though barely out of her first trimester, her belly had ballooned in size the last week and none of her clothes fit.

"Go naked then," Azarius said, wrapping his arms around her and nuzzling her neck.

"I can't do that," she said, turning to kiss him. "Your mother will be there, remember?"

"Oh, right. Well, then how about that maxi dress you wore a few weeks ago? It was stretchy, right? It's supposed to warmer today, and we'll be inside anyway."

"That is a great idea. I knew I married you for a reason." She flashed him a smile and then bounced into the closet to grab the dress.

"I thought it was my mysterious allure," he called from behind her.

Lanie popped her head out of the closet. "No, that I always hated, remember?"

Azarius laughed. "My rugged good looks?"

Lanie tugged the dress over her head. It sat a little off kilter with her baby bump, but it looked okay. "Yes, those I love," she said walking back to him and tilting her face up to kiss him again. "Now, we better go or we're going to be late."

The barn was already packed when they arrived. A huge banner that read "Congratulations Azarius and Lanie" hung across the front door. Layla had insisted on throwing them both a "belated wedding" party and a "congratulations on the new baby" party." Lanie had convinced her to throw them both at the same time. Because Layla had asked, nearly the whole town had shown up.

Of course, it probably helped that the town had officially adopted Lanie and Azarius into the fold. Even the few staunch grinches had changed their tune when Azarius began helping the local businesses with a marketing plan that had drawn more tourists this past summer than ever before.

She and Azarius had even officially taken over

Perkins from her father and increased revenue so much that they'd hired a few local teens to take the afternoon shift, leaving Lanie time to write and Azarius time to run the advertising.

"Hey bro, long time no see," Greg, no longer on crutches, but still limping slightly embraced Azarius as soon as they opened the door. With him was a stunning, petite woman with dark hair and the greenest eyes Lanie had ever seen.

"Lanie, you look amazing," Greg said, embracing her next. "I want you to meet Jada, and while I don't want to steal your thunder, I did want to share we just got engaged last night."

"Oh that's wonderful," Lanie said as Azarius issued congratulations as well. Greg looked happier than she could remember seeing him, and as she shook Jada's hand, she had a feeling their relationship would be a good one.

Before they could take another step farther into the barn, a stout woman with long blond hair gathered Azarius into a hug. Mary, this had to be Mary. Though they'd spoken on the phone, Lanie had yet to meet her mother-in-law as Mary didn't travel very often.

"It's good to see you too, Mother," Azarius said. "I would like you to meet Lanie."

Mary turned warm brown eyes on her, and Lanie could see why Azarius confided in his mother. She had a presence like warm cookies on Christmas Day that just made you want to spill everything.

"It's so nice to meet you," Lanie said, holding out her hand, but Mary pulled her in for a hug.

"It's nice to meet the woman who's finally completed my son. I knew when he first talked about you that you were special, but seeing you - I can see that you two were made for each other."

Lanie smiled at Azarius and squeezed his hand.

Her parents came next, and Lanie was surprised to see a smile on her father's face as he approached.

"I have to say I had my doubts, but you have proven to be a good man, Azarius," her father said, shaking Azarius's hand.

"Thank you, sir. That means a lot coming from you."

"And we know it's early," her mother said, "but we brought you a baby gift to say congratulations. I know you don't know the gender of the baby yet, but I know babies love loveys, so…" She pulled a bright yellow ducky out of the bag she was holding.

"Oh, it looks just like my old lovey," Lanie sighed. "Thank you, Mother."

"You are welcome, Dear. We're so proud of you both."

Her parents moved along, and more guests approached to issue well wishes - Bert and Amelia (who were evidently back together after their break), Barnard, Paula, Presley and Brandon, and people whose names Lanie wasn't even sure she knew. Layla and Max brought up the rear.

"Thank you for this party, Layla," Azarius said. "You went above and beyond."

"Well, I was happy to do it, though I'm not sure why we had to do it on this specific day." Layla said pointedly at Lanie.

Lanie smiled and shook her head. That was a secret only for her and Azarius.

"Why did you pick my birthday for this party?" Azarius whispered when they were out of ear shot of everyone else.

"I thought you needed a happy memory for once around it," Lanie said. "I didn't tell anyone else, so we don't have to make a big deal about it."

Azarius pulled her in for an unexpected hug. "You are amazing, Lanie. Did you know that?"

Lanie laughed as she squeezed him back. "Okay, I'm amazing. Can we go sit now? My feet are killing me?"

"Almost," he said.

Music flooded the barn, and he led her to the center of the dance floor.

"I thought you didn't dance in public," she said with a smile as she locked her arms around his neck.

"There are a lot of things I do now that I didn't do before," he said, turning her in a slow circle. "Like sharing a house."

Lanie smiled. "Good thing you got over that one because it won't be much longer before it's even fuller. Oh, I finished the book by the way."

He tilted his head. "What book?"

"Our story, silly. You told me the day we eloped that Lanie Jacobson sounded like a good author's name, so I decided to try it out. I've been writing in the afternoons while you market, and I think I finally finished it."

"That's amazing, Lanie. What's it called?"

"Love Conquers All," she said.

He nodded slowly. "Love Conquers All," he said. "I like it. It's a good title."

"No," Lanie said with a shake of her head. "It's a great title. It means everything."

Azarius smiled and pulled her closer. "It means everything."

The End!

NOT READY TO SAY GOODBYE YET?

Love Conquers All is the last book in the Star Lake series so far, but that doesn't mean the fun has to end. How would you like to check out another great series.

The Lawkeeper series has five books. Three historical and two contemporary stories and all of them follow a lawman of some kind. So, put on your cowboy hats and badges and say hello to Jesse Jennings and Kate Whitby

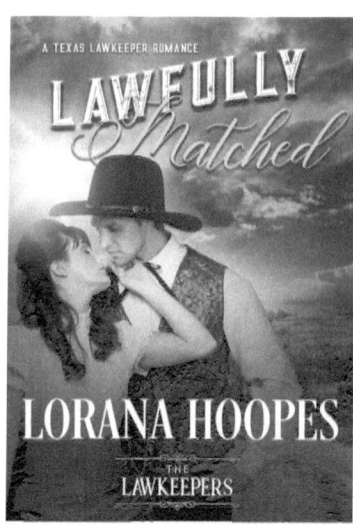

Lawfully Matched

He's reeling from the death of his betrothed...

Jesse Jennings wanted nothing to do with the law until a group of bandits killed his betrothed. Now, he's out for vengeance, but Kate Whidby stands in his way.

She thought she was marrying a rancher....

Kate Whidby left Boston when her parents died in search of a life out west, but when the man she agreed to marry turns out to not be what he portrayed, she must find a way to escape.

Timing changes everything....

He's without a wife. She's without a home or money. Will they find love through this marriage of convenience?

Read of for a sneak peek at Lawfully Matched....

*B*oston, Massachusetts 1883

Mary Katherine Whidby grabbed the local paper and strolled to a corner to read in private. While she hated to leave her beloved Boston, she was quickly approaching the spinster age, and all the surrounding men seemed intimidated by her brains or more likely her strong-willed spirit as her brother Robert liked to remind her.

Mary Katherine, or Kate as her family called her, had always held a grand notion of love, so agreeing to marry a complete stranger caused distaste in her mouth every time she thought about it, but her options had run out when her parents died.

She opened the paper and scanned the offerings:

'Forty-year-old widowed rancher looking for wife who can be a mother to three kids.'

Three kids? Kate shook her head and drew a line through that one. While she wanted kids one day, she did not feel confident stepping into the role immediately.

'Fifty-year-old Pastor seeks wife for companionship and to lead women's socials at local church.'

A pastor's wife wouldn't be too bad, but the age difference was more than Kate could stomach. After all, she was barely twenty-five, which would make this man twice her age, and wasn't the lifespan shorter in the west? Knowing her luck, he would die shortly after she arrived, and she'd be left all alone.

'Thirty-year-old saloon owner seeks wife and possible waitress.'

While this one was closer in age, Kate had no desire, or skills for that matter, to work in a saloon.

The pickings were slim this month it seemed. Just one ad left.

'Thirty-two-year-old farmer in search of brave woman to help on homestead.'

Well, she didn't know much about farming, but no one would say Kate wasn't brave. She had even taken shooting lessons with her brother and father.

Crossing her fingers this man would not be a con man or an abuser, she made her way to the counter.

"Hello Miss Kate, what can I help you with today?" Mr. Gaines, the elderly owner of the newspaper asked. He wore a black vest over his shirt and a pair of old spectacles sat on the bridge of his nose.

Kate cleared her throat, still embarrassed to be doing this. "I wanted to inquire how I might go about answering an ad."

"Hmm, let me see," he said, pushing up his glasses as he read the ad. "Mail-order bride?" He looked up at Kate. "Does that mean we're losing you?"

A heated flush flared across Kate's face. "Well, there isn't much left for me here with mother and father gone."

"Don't you still have a brother?" Mr. Gaines asked kindly.

Kate nodded. "I do, but Robert just married, and he's trying to get his practice up and running. I would just be in the way." She didn't add the fact that his wife Abigail appeared to despise her, and the thought of staying in their house much longer held little appeal.

"Well, if you're sure," he said, though the tone of his voice told her he wasn't convinced. He reached below the cabinet and pulled out a pad of paper and a pencil. "Generally, you write the man back and see if it's a good fit."

"Oh," Kate stammered. She had not realized she would need to reply. "Thank you," she said taking the paper and pencil. "I will return this shortly."

Kate headed back to the corner and sat down at the table, thinking for a moment. She placed the pencil on the paper and scribbled out:

D*ear Mr. Easterly,*
 My name is Kate Whidby. I am a brave twenty-five-year-old woman with dark hair and blue eyes. I am looking for love and adventure in a new area. I saw your ad in my paper, and although I do not know much about farming, I am a quick study and think I could be the woman you are looking for. Please advise if this is acceptable. I would like to travel as soon as possible.
 Kate Whidby

. . .

S he folded the letter and returned to Mr. Gaines. "Do you have an envelope I could use to send this?"

Mr. Gaines supplied one from under the counter and handed it to her. Kate quickly jotted her name and address down and sealed the envelope. She held it out to Mr. Gaines, but he shook his head.

"Take it to the post office. They will send it out and your response will come back through them."

"How long do you think it will take to get a reply?"

"I don't know for sure, but my guess would be about two weeks."

Kate's jaw dropped open. "Two weeks?"

Mr. Gaines nodded and scratched the side of his bald head with the back of the pencil. "Yes ma'am, unless you'd like to telegraph it. That costs considerably more though."

Kate fingered the few coins she had managed to find in her parent's bedroom as she was packing up the last items she'd been able to take. No, she had better be frugal and spend only a little.

"No, two weeks is fine." Perhaps, she could find a temporary job. It would be nice to have some money for the trip.

Kate paid the small fee and left with the letter in

hand. After a quick stop in the post office to drop it off, she continued on to the mercantile to pick up a few items.

Once inside the store, she loaded the basket with the necessities—flour, sugar, teas—and then picked up a few pieces of penny candy. Kate felt guilty for imposing on Robert and Abigail by staying with them at their house, especially so early in their marriage, but her parents had rented their house. Kate took care for her parents but had no money to continue the payments after their death, and so she had been forced to give up her home.

"Morning, Miss Kate," Sally, the plump owner of the Mercantile, smiled at her.

Kate had often wondered how Sally had married before she did, but then she would remember the two marriage proposals she had turned down. Funny how she had rebuffed those proposals because she felt she didn't know the men well enough, yet now she was planning to travel across the country and marry a man she'd never met.

"Hello, Sally," she said, laying the items on the counter. "How is business?"

"It is not too bad," Sally said. Then she glanced behind her and leaned forward. "Tell you the truth, it has been a little slow the last few months. John is stressed about it," she whispered.

Kate smiled and leaned in to reply. "Well, I will keep praying it will pick up."

"That is mighty kind of you, Kate. Will I see you at church on Sunday?"

Kate nodded, but the question sent her mind spinning. God was an important part of her life. Would there be proper churches in Texas?

S age Creek, Texas 1883

J esse Jennings removed his hat and wiped the sweat from his brow. Finally, the last fence post was in. With his cattle safe once again, he would now be able to focus on putting the finishing touches on his homestead, so he could marry Pauline.

As he replaced his hat, Sheriff Johnson rode up. Jesse sighed and lifted his gaze to the lawman.

"What can I do for you, Sheriff?" he asked, though he knew the answer to the question. Sheriff Johnson had come around once every few days like clockwork over the past month, trying to enlist Jessie as a deputy sheriff.

Jesse enjoyed the protection the law provided as much as the next person, but he was just a simple rancher, and all he wanted to do was marry his sweetheart and raise cattle.

Unfortunately, time and money had dwindled after some rough winter weather and the previous summer's drought, extending the finishing of the homestead.

"You know why I'm here, Jesse," the older man said as he dismounted his chocolate brown stallion. "There was another robbery last night. This time at Doc Moore's office. No one was hurt, but they took a lot of his supplies. We need more men to help patrol. At least until we catch these varmints." He removed his hat and ran his leathery hand through his salt-and-pepper hair.

"I'm sorry to hear that Sheriff, but as I've told you before, I'm not a lawman, and I need to finish this homestead."

Sheriff Johnson planted his hands on his slim hips and donned his hat again. "Well, I can set with that, but the attacks appear to be becoming more frequent. I just hope you still have a home when all is said and done."

With that, Sheriff Johnson tipped the brim of his black Stetson before re-mounting his horse.

Jesse lifted a hand in a loose wave and watched the sheriff recede from view. Maybe Sheriff Johnson was right. He was young, in shape, and not half bad with a gun.

Once he finished the homestead he'd be able to think about it. Right now, thoughts of Pauline with her long blonde hair consumed his thoughts.

Jesse checked the sun on the horizon. It had sunk low, leaving the sky a brilliant orange and pink color. He had lost track of time and needed to wash up before dinner with his fiancée.

Keep reading Lawfully Matched.

THE STORY DOESN'T END!

You've met a few people and fallen in love....

I bet you're wondering how you can meet everyone else.

Star Lake Series:
When Love Returns
Once Upon a Star
Love Conquers All
Heartbeats Series:
Where It All Began
The Power of Prayer
When Hearts Collide
A Past Forgiven
Sweet Billionaires Series:

The Billionaire's Secret

Brush with a Billionaire

The Billionaire's Christmas Miracle

The Billionaire's Cowboy Groom

The Lawkeepers series:

Lawfully Matched

Lawfully Justified

The Scarlet Wedding

Lawfully Redeemed

Lawfully Pursued

Stand alones:

The Still Small Voice

Love Renewed

Blushing Brides Series:

The Cowboy's Reality Bride

The Reality Bride's Baby

The Producer's Unlikely Bride

Her children's early reader chapter book series:

The Wishing Stone #1: Dangerous Dinosaur

The Wishing Stone #2: Dragon Dilemma

The Wishing Stone #3: Mesmerizing Mermaids

The Wishing Stone #4: Pyramid Puzzles

The Wishing Stone Inspirations #1: Mary's Miracle

To see a list of all her books

authorloranahoopes.com
loranahoopes@gmail.com

WOULD YOU LEAVE A REVIEW?

As an author, I highly appreciate the feedback I get from my readers. It helps others make an informed decision before buying my book. If you enjoyed this book, please leave a review at your retailer.

Do you like free books? I'm offering a free sample of my next book Free Sample!

ABOUT THE AUTHOR

Lorana Hoopes is an inspirational author originally from Texas but now living in the PNW with her husband and three children. When not writing, she can be seen kickboxing at the gym, singing, or acting on stage. One day, she hopes to retire from teaching and write full time.

If you enjoyed this story, be sure to check out Lorana's other books.

When Love Returns: The first in the Star Lake series. Presley Hays and Brandon Scott were best friends in High School until Morgan entered their town and stole Brandon's heart. Devastated, Presley takes a scholarship to Le Cordon Bleu, but five years later, she is back in Star Lake after a tough breakup. Brandon thought he'd never return to Star Lake after Morgan left him and his daughter Joy, but when his father needs help, he returns home and finds more than he bargained for. Can Presley and Brandon forget past hurts or will their stubborn natures keep them apart forever? http://books2read.com/whenlovereturns

Once Upon a Star: The second book in the Star Lake series. Audrey left Star Lake to pursue acting, but after an unplanned pregnancy her jobs and her

money dwindled, leaving her no option except to return home and start over. Blake was the quintessential nerd in high school and was never able to tell Audrey how he felt. Now that he's gained confidence and some muscle, will he finally be able to reveal his feelings? Once Upon a Star will take you back to Christmas in Star Lake. Revisit your favorite characters and meet a few ones in this sweet Christmas read.
https://www.books2read.com/OUAStar

Love Conquers All: Lanie Perkins Hall never imagined being divorced at thirty. Nor did she imagine falling for an old friend, but when she runs into Azarius Jacobson, she can't deny the attraction. As they begin to spend more time together, Lanie struggles with the fact Azarius keeps his past a secret. What is he hiding? And will she ever be able to get him to open up? Azarius Jacobson has loved Lanie Perkins Hall from the moment he saw her, but issues from his past have left him guarded. Now that he has another chance with her, will he find the courage to share his life with her? Or will his emotional walls create a barrier that will leave him alone once more? Find out in this heartfelt, emotional third book (stand alone) in the Star Lake series.

https://www.books2read.com/loveconquersall

Where It All Began: Sandra Baker thought her life was on the right track until she ended up pregnant. Her boyfriend, not wanting the baby, pushes her to have an abortion. After the procedure, Sandra's life falls apart, and she turns to alcohol. Her relationship ends, and she struggles to find meaning in her life. When she meets Henry Dobbs, a strong Christian man, she begins to wonder if God would accept her. Will she tell Henry her darkest secret? And will she ever be able to forgive herself and find healing? Find out in this emotional love story. http://books2read.com/WhereBegan

The Power of Prayer: Callie Green thought she had her whole life planned out until her fiance left her at the altar. When her carefully laid plans crumble, she begins to make mistakes at work and engage in uncharacteristic activities. After a mistake nearly costs her her job, she cashes in her honeymoon tickets for some time away. There she meets JD, a charming Christian man who, even though she is not a believer, captures her interest. Before their relationship can deepen, Callie's ex-fiance shows back

up in her life and she is forced to choose between Daniel and JD. Who will she choose and how will her choice affect the rest of her life? Find out in this touching   novel.
http://books2read.com/PowerofPrayer

When Hearts Collide: Amanda Adams has always been a Christian, but she's a novice at relationships. When she meets Caleb, her emotions get the best of her and she ignores the sign that something is amiss. Will she find out before it's too late? Jared Masterson is still healing from his girlfriend's strange rejection and disappearance when he meets Amanda. She captivates his heart, but can he save her from making the biggest mistake of her life? A must read for mothers and daughters. Though part of the series and the first of the college spin off series, it is a stand alone book and can be read separately.
http://books2read.com/Whenheartscollide

A Past Forgiven: Jess Peterson has lived a life of abuse and lost her self worth, but when she is paired with a Christian roommate, she begins to wonder if there is a loving father looking down on her. Her decisions lead her one way, but when she ends up pregnant, she must make some major changes. Chad

Michelson is healing from his own past and uses meaningless relationships to hide his pain, but when Jess becomes pregnant, he begins to wonder about the meaning of life. Can he step up and be there for Jess and the baby? http://books2read.com/APF

A Father's Love: Maxwell Banks was the ultimate player until he found himself caring for a daughter he didn't know he had. Can he change to become the role model she needs? Alyssa Miller hasn't had the best luck with past relationships, so why is she falling for the one man who is sure to break her heart? Though nearly complete opposites, feelings develop, but can Max really change his philandering ways? Or will one mistake seal his fate forever? http://books2read.com/AFathersLove

A Brush with a Billionaire: Brent just wanted to finish his novel in peace, but when his car breaks down in Sweet Grove, he is forced to deal with a female mechanic and try to get along. Sam thought she had given up on city boys, but when Brent shows up in her shop, she finds herself fighting attraction. Will their stubborn natures keep them apart or can a small town festival bring them together? http://books2read.com/bwab

Lawfully Matched: Kate Whidby doesn't want to impose on her newly married brother after their parents die, so she accepts a mail order bride offer in the paper. Little does she know the man she intends to marry has a dark past, sending her fleeing into a neighboring town and into Jesse Jenning's life. Jesse never wanted to be in law enforcement, but after a band of robbers kills his fiancee, he dons the badge and swears revenge. Will he find his fiancee's killer? And when Kate flies into his life, will he be able to put his painful past behind him in order to love again? http://books2read.com/lawfullymatched

Lawfully Justified

William Cook enjoyed serving the town as a lawman until a tragic accident took everything he loved. Wanting to leave his past behind, he turns to bounty hunting, enjoying the constant distraction—and the money isn't too bad either. When he suffers a life-threatening injury, he is forced to stay put for longer than he is used to doing. The woman who tends his wounds intrigues him, but he isn't looking for love after what happened the first time.

Emma Stewart recently lost her husband and has moved back in with her widowed father, the town doctor. While she likes helping him heal the sick, she still longs for a family of her own, so no one is more surprised than she is when she starts to develop feeling for the bounty hunter, who hides his heart of gold behind a rugged exterior.

Can Emma offer William a reason to stay? Can William find a way to heal from his broken past to start a future with Emma? Or will a haunting secret take away all the possibilities of this budding romance? http://books2read.com/LawfullyJustified

The Still Small Voice: Jordan Wright was searching for something after she gave her son up for adoption. What she found was God, and she began receiving visions. But can she trust Him when he asks her to do something big? Kat Jameson had long been a lukewarm Christian, but when her friend dies and she begins seeing lights, she thinks she is going crazy. Then she meets someone with a message for her. Will she be able to give up control and do what is asked of her? http://books2read.com/tssv

Her children's early reader chapter book series:

The Wishing Stone #1: Dangerous Dinosaur http://books2read.com/WishingStone1

The Wishing Stone #2: Dragon Dilemma
http://books2read.com/WishingStone2

The Wishing Stone #3: Mesmerizing Mermaids
http://books2read.com/wishingstone3

The Wishing Stone #4: Pyramid Puzzle COMING
SOON

authorloranahoopes.com
loranahoopes@gmail.com